What Doesn't
Break Us

What Doesn't Break Us

SONIA RODRIGUEZ

TATE PUBLISHING
AND **ENTERPRISES**, LLC

Published by Tate Publishing & Enterprises, LLC
127 E. Trade Center Terrace | Mustang, Oklahoma 73064 USA
1.888.361.9473 | www.tatepublishing.com

Tate Publishing is committed to excellence in the publishing industry. The company reflects the philosophy established by the founders, based on Psalm 68:11,
"The Lord gave the word and great was the company of those who published it."

Book design copyright © 2016 by Tate Publishing, LLC. All rights reserved.
Cover design by Samson Lim
Interior design by Richell Balansag

Published in the United States of America

ISBN: 978-1-68293-662-7
1. Fiction / Romance / General
2. Fiction / Hispanic & Latino
16.02.15

Contents

Acknowledgement

I wanted to thank first and foremost my God Almighty for paving the way to see one of my dreams become a reality.

To my first audience and guinea pig, my oldest son Carlos. You were ten years old when I first decided to start writing. As the adventures of Celia and Nando unfolded, you patiently sat with me night after night to listen, offer suggestions and support. I love you with all my heart.

To my youngest son, Hunter. You are like a full grown size version of "Yoda". Your insight and inexplicable wisdom has spoken to me during times where I doubted my own abilities. I'm in awe at the wonderful man you are becoming and I thank you for being my sidekick.

To my beautiful daughter Tatianna. How can I have been so lucky to have you? From beauty tips to boys, we have the most wonderful and unique relationship. I thank you for loving me unconditionally and being there during times when I was not at my best.

My mom, Ana. I have without a doubt the best mother in the world. You have rejoiced during my triumphs and suffered right alongside me, even when living in another state! We need to remedy this distance soon. I love you and I'm forever thankful for the richness that you have brought into my life and the lives of my children.

My cousin Elaine. You always keep my best childhood memories alive. You have brought much needed laughs and smiles when at times I felt I couldn't do either.

My adoptive family, my friends. The list is long but solid. To each of you, for pouring into my soul, listening and counseling, I have nothing but love and the greatest respect.

Last but not least, my grandparents. Your journey set the platform for my overall outlook on life. You taught me to always be a lady. I will forever wear a slip, carry a purse with Kleenex, lipstick and enough money to get me out of a jam. I will never stop learning and I will forever believe that my faith and confidence in myself will get me through anything in life.

Puerto Rico has been a possession of the United States for more than a century, but it has never been a state.

Its people have been US citizens since 1917, and as such, they can move throughout the fifty states just as any American can.

Although the US tried to promote Puerto Rico as a glamorous tourist destination, in the early twentieth century, the island suffered severe economic depression.

This led to many islanders eager for a fresh start.

US factory owners and employment agencies had begun recruiting heavily on the island. In addition, the postwar years saw the return home of thousands of Puerto Rican war veterans, whose service in the US military had shown them the world.

After centuries of immigration by boat, the Puerto Rican migration became the first great airborne migration in US history.

Book I
Celia

Penuelas, Puerto Rico, 1941

The door slammed behind her. Her father, Juan Luis, was home.

Celia didn't even flinch as she went about washing the rice.

"Mmmm, something smells delicious," her father slurred. "What are we having?" Celia could smell the stench of stale cigars and liquor on his unwashed body, even before he stumbled his way into the kitchen.

Her father came to stand next to her and uncovered the pot of simmering beans on the stove. Celia cringed as she tried to continue with her task.

The savory vapors escaped the pot of beans, and her dad took a whiff. "Is that ham in there?" he asked Celia.

She looked up and said, "Yes, Papa. Momma says ham makes the beans tastier. I have some chicken in the oven, and the rice should be ready in about twenty minutes."

She learned to cook by watching her mom. And although she knew she would never be as good of a cook as her mom was, what she managed to make was at the very least…edible. Or so she thought, judging by her father's grunts at dinnertime.

"Well, nena," her father said, "there may be some use for you after all."

"What do you mean?" Celia asked with unease. Her father was always verbally abusive.

Her father approached her and cupped her chin in his hands. Celia looked into her father's bloodshot eyes and tried in vain to control her nausea as her father's rancid breath invaded every pore of her being.

"Celia, Celia, no man is going to marry you. I hate to tell you this because you're my daughter, but you're not very pretty. You have teeth as big as a horse, the nose of a pig, and the eyes of a cow." Then he had a sudden bout of laughter, which he tried to contain.

Celia looked at her father, disgusted by the snot running out of his nose and the spit coming down the side of his mouth, and she couldn't help but wonder why he hated her so. She turned away and poured the rice into the boiling water. She swallowed in vain to contain her stomach.

Juan Luis laughed so hard that he almost missed the chair as he sat down. "We have the whole farm under one roof," he said in between laughs.

She excused herself and went to the bathroom. She bent over the sink and threw up. She turned on the faucet to wash away what looked like chunks of apples. She scooped some water in her hands and rinsed out her mouth.

Then she splashed water on her face. She patted her face dry just like her momma showed her.

She stared at her image in the mirror. Her long brown hair cascaded in waves around her face and stopped in the middle of her back.

She opened her dark-brown oval-shaped eyes wide and then squinted them. Yes, she thought, her eyes were too big for her face.

Next she smiled big and got closer to the mirror. She examined her teeth for a brief minute, and then she closed her mouth. Her lips seem to overpower the bottom half of her face. She sucked in her cheeks. With her large eyes, she resembled a fish.

Celia was shorter than most girls her age. In that aspect, she had no clue whom she took after, because her mother was five feet nine and her dad was well over six feet. Maybe she'll have a growth spurt at some point. She was roughly about 125 pounds. Her figure curved in places she wished it didn't. Her waist appeared supersmall and out of proportion with her hips. Her breasts started coming in about three months after she first got her period, at age twelve. She was now fifteen, and her breasts didn't seem to have grown any more in the last three years.

It made her uncomfortable when boys would look at her and stare. She was not pretty at all, so she wasn't sure why she gained so much attention from them. Her father was right, she would be lucky if anyone would want to marry her someday.

She put up her towel, turned off the light, and walked out of the bathroom.

She made her way back to the kitchen, praying and hoping that her father had passed out.

She was pleasantly surprised to find that her father had indeed fallen asleep and was now snoring loudly. But more so at the sight of her mother stirring the rice.

Her mother turned around and instantly smiled when she saw her daughter. "There you are, my precious! I was wondering where you were. The rice is done." She wiped her hands on her skirt and opened her arms for Celia.

Celia made a mad dash to her mother's waiting arms. She closed her eyes and inhaled deeply and succumbed to the scent of lilies. Her mother always smelled so good. She opened her eyes and saw that her mom still had on her name tag. It read *Iluminada*. It was a wonderful name. It meant the Enlightened One.

Her mother kissed her hair. "How was your day?"

"It was good," Celia lied. She was too embarrassed to tell her mother about what her dad had said to her earlier.

Her mother didn't look convinced but decided that she would talk to Celia after dinner.

Celia helped her mom prep the table for dinner and serve supper. By then, Juan Luis had awoken from his cat nap, and the trio ate in silence.

Throughout the course of the meal, Iluminada gestured for her daughter's attention by kicking her under the table.

Celia looked up and saw that her mom was gesturing with her eyes toward her dad. Then she wrinkled her nose like she had smelled a skunk. She then crossed her eyes and stuck out her tongue as if she was imitating roadkill.

Celia looked down at her food and shook violently, trying to contain her laughter. But when she looked at her mom again, she completely lost it. Then both mom and daughter started laughing out loud.

Her father looked up at both his wife and daughter and decided that they had lost their minds. "What's wrong with the two of you?" When no one responded, he shouted, "Quiet, I say!"

Celia and her mom quieted down. Her dad threw down his napkin, got up and looked at both of them with disgust, and stormed out of the room, muttering some cuss words and something about being cursed to live with disrespectful women.

When Juan Luis was well out of earshot, they both started laughing all over again, tears streaming down both of their faces. Oh…Celia's belly ached, and it felt so good to feel carefree. Her mother always made her laugh, and she loved her so much.

They cleared the dishes from the table. They usually cleaned up the kitchen together unless her dad called her mom to have a private talk. She knew they didn't do much talking when they shut their door.

Her friends, the brother-sister duo of Elizondo and Marife, explained what grown-ups do behind closed doors. It seems they had caught their parents a couple of times in that horrible compromising way.

Celia hoped that tonight her father would not call for her mother. She knew her mom had little to no respect for her dad, and at times, she felt sorry for her mom.

Maybe at one time, her father was a good supportive husband and father. But everything changed when he lost his job.

Juan Luis was a farmer. He owned a little piece of land where he grew a variety of fruits and vegetables, such as oranges, mangoes, quenepas, lemons, tomatoes, and a variety of peppers. He had several men working for him who would help collect and sort through the crop and load them into a buggy for distribution and sale to the local businesses. But it all changed when Hurricane San Ciprian crossed the entire length of the island of Puerto Rico.

They say the hurricane was a Category 4 in strength— this being one level below the highest category there is, with winds reaching up to 156 miles per hour. The overall damage to the island was catastrophic.

For Celia's hometown, Penuelas, as it was located on the southern coast of the island, homes and business were lost on the lower ground with the overflow of the three rivers that cross the towns Guayanes, Macana, and Tallaboa.

The storms left millions of dollars in agricultural damage for citrus, sugar, coffee, tobacco, and honey harvest—in addition to the loss in livestock.

In the end, Hurricane San Ciprian killed about 257 people, injured 4,280 more, and left around 500 homeless.

Soon after, the US National Guard was sent to help the injured and the homeless. The American Red Cross also helped in distributing food and medical equipment.

President Herbert Hoover, along with local officials, set up several relief committees to raise funds and encourage residents to continue the cleanup efforts.

Celia lived in a modest wooden house with a roof made of corrugated metal sheets called zinc. The house was one of about eight houses that were built on a hill.

Due to its location, water damage was minimal as the houses were far up from the ground. But some of the roofs had been badly damaged or completely torn off due to the high winds of the hurricane.

Celia's roof had been damaged to the point where it appeared that some gigantic hand had tried to open her house as if it were a can of sardines. Half of her roof had come off the wooden posts and curled inward. This left the back rooms exposed, meaning her room and her parents' room and part of the bathroom. This forced her family to set up camp in their living room. Celia had been six years old at the time and barely remembered, but her mother would retell the story for years to come.

So amid the tragedies, the townsfolk came together, and as donations and supplies of all kinds overflowed the island and her town, Celia's home soon had a new roof.

Her mom said that God always finds a way to provide us with what we need, when we need it the most. All we have to do is…have faith.

Her father was never able to build up the business or recuperate any of his loses. So he became a regular at a local bar and drank his days away.

"Iluminada!" her father bellowed. She looked at her mom. Her serene look was now transformed to one of pure irritation.

"It's okay, Momma," she said. "I'll finish up."

Her mom threw the rag that she had been using into the sink. She took off her apron and hung it from the doorknob of the pantry.

With a look of regret, she kissed Celia on her forehead. "Don't forget to brush your teeth. Okay?"

"Okay, Momma."

Celia dried off the dishes one by one. She realized that some of them were chipped at the edges.

The silverware was equally worn. Some of the spoons were bent, and there was only one sharp knife in the drawer.

Her family was, what some might say, poor. Her mother, who provided the only income for the family, put herself through night school while working during the day as a seamstress at a small local dress store before Celia was born.

Her mom had hand-made virtually everything in their home from scraps the store discarded. She had made all the curtains and bedspreads. She had even sewed Celia's clothes. And despite the lack of luxuries, Celia's mom had made their home warm and inviting.

Iluminada had become a certified midwife despite her dad's lack of support. He always berated her mom for not tending to him and always saying that a woman's place was at home, not out gallivanting.

"Where have you been, cabrona?" he would say.

Momma, accustomed to the inquiry, would just calmly reply, "I was at the Dedo's residence. Silvia just delivered a healthy baby boy. It was a hard pregnancy, but thank God, everything turned out all right."

"Bah excuses! Always excuses! I know what you've been up to. I have seen the way men look at you," her father would say. But ignoring his comments, Mom would continue detailing us with the events of the birth.

Regardless of what her dad said, her mom always found time for them.

On particularly long nights when her mom was called away because someone was going to have a baby, Celia would wait up and make hot cocoa for the both of them. When her mom came home, she would tell her all about the new baby she helped bring to the world.

"Felicia had twins!"

Celia opened her eyes wide. "No way! You said she would, and the husband thought you were crazy, remember?"

"I know, I know."

"So what were they? Boys? Girls?"

Celia's mom had a sneaky smile. "Guess."

"Oh, Mom, tell me…"

"Okay, okay. She had…oh, what was it? I can't think now…It's so late…"

"Mom!" Celia said with mock exasperation.

Her mom laughed. "It was a boy *and* a girl."

Celia laughed too. "Her husband is probably thinking you cursed him."

"Probably so. He will probably tell his friends I'm a witch! That's okay, though…I need the rest," Iluminada said.

Celia stopped laughing because something in her mom's tone didn't feel right. She studied her mom's face and noticed she looked exhausted. She also had dark circles under her eyes.

She was about to suggest to her mom to take some time off, when her mom suddenly jumped up and said, "Oh, I almost forgot to give you this!" Her mom went to the closet and brought out a package and handed it over to Celia.

"What is it, Momma?" Celia opened the package quickly to find what appeared to be a piece of white cloth. As she unfolded it, the cloth took shape of the most beautiful dress she had ever seen.

"Oh, Momma…" She was speechless.

"I was hoping to have it done sooner, but you know... Go ahead try it on." Iluminada motioned with her hand.

Celia took her off pajamas, and her mom helped her button the dress. She then stepped back and looked at Celia with a critical eye. "Mmm...I don't know. It seems like it's missing something. Okay, hold on right there. I'll be back."

Her mom came back and asked Celia to turn around. She pinned Celia's hair up high and then proceeded to place something around Celia's neck. When Celia turned around, her mom had the biggest smile she had ever seen, and she appeared to be on the verge of tears.

Celia looked down and saw her mother's wearing pearls dangling from her neck. "Momma, this is yours. I may lose it."

"Nonsense, Celia. It is yours now. You are the most beautiful creature that I have ever seen, and you deserve to have it."

"I love you, Momma," Celia said, choking back tears.

Mother and daughter embraced for a long time. Engulfed in her mother's sweet fragrance of lilies, Celia had felt protected. She loved that scent.

She remembered going to bed thinking and knowing that no matter what she really did look like, her mother loved her unconditionally.

Her mother had been the only one to teach her how to smile.

2

Life for Celia was routine.

Ever since she could remember, she had been on her own. She went to school. Came home. Did homework. Did her chores and helped with dinner.

If her father happened to be home by the time she left for school, he was usually passed out, sleeping away his night binge.

Her mom had to be at the dress store by 4:00 a.m., and if she was summoned to deliver a baby or make her routine visits to the expecting mothers, then she wouldn't be home until late.

Her father never allowed any of her friends to come over, which was fine by Celia, who didn't really care to explain her drunken father to anyone.

He was always verbally abusive, and sometimes Celia wished she could just punch him hard in the face. She was ashamed of such thoughts as she was taught to always respect her elders.

On one particular day, she came home from school and noticed her mom's purse in the foyer leading to the living room. She was immediately ecstatic at the idea that her mom was home early. This meant that they would be having some sort of sugary delicacy for supper. On the rare occasions that her mom came home early, she always baked for them. It was a wonderful treat, and Celia looked forward to it all the time.

She dropped her backpack and made her way to the kitchen, sure to find her mother covered in flour and singing out of tune to some made-up melody.

When she walked into the kitchen, she saw her mother on the kitchen floor. Celia dropped to her knees next to her mother's figure. She shook her and yelled, "Mama! Mama!" But no response.

In a panic, Celia rushed outside to get her neighbor Esperanza.

Esperanza and Legran Muniz had known Celia since she was a baby. Their only son had been killed in the war, so Celia became like a daughter to them.

They weren't allowed to visit either, on account of Legran giving Juan Luis a piece of his mind and almost coming to blows with him when Legran witnessed his treatment of Celia. But, nonetheless, they checked on Celia from time to time to make sure she was all right.

After repeated desperate knocks from Celia, Esperanza finally shouted, "Ya voy…un momentito."

She opened the door to find a pale Celia speaking incoherently and crying. Esperanza had to ask Celia several times to calm down. "*Que te pasa, niña?*" "What's wrong?"

"It's Mama," Celia cried. "I can't wake her…"

Esperanza yelled out to her husband, Legran, and they both rushed to Celia's house. Unable to wake Iluminada, Legran left to fetch the only doctor in town, leaving a worried wife and an inconsolable Celia.

Dear God, he thought, *what is going to be of this child if she loses her mother?*

Soon after the doctor arrived, Iluminada came to. The men lifted her and placed her on her bed. The doctor asked to speak with her privately.

Celia was a wreck.

It seemed like hours before the doctor came out of the room. He went directly to Celia.

"How's Momma? What's wrong with her?" Celia asked.

Dr. Samuel Fuentes looked at this wide-eyed loving girl and wished that he could shield her for what was to come. He too had known Celia since she was a baby. And it was no secret in their small little town that her father was a drunken mess and was abusive toward his wife and child.

At one time, he and Juan Luis were friends. He had even offered financial support to help Juan Luis regain his business. But Juan Luis was too prideful and refused his friend's generosity.

Juan Luis went as far as to accuse Samuel of being in love with his wife, Iluminada.

The friendship ended on a sour note. And he had not spoken to Juan Luis or Iluminada until she came to his office about six months ago.

Iluminada had complained of feeling fatigued and in pain all the time. She thought it was on account of her long hours. And after close examination, he knew what they were up against.

And now the moment had come to tell Celia the truth. With false courage, the doctor took a deep breath. "Your mom...Celia...your mom has tuberculosis."

"So is she going to be okay? Can you cure her?" Celia asked, hopeful. But she knew what the T word meant. It was certain death. She was old enough to know that much.

"I'm afraid, Celia, the disease is in her lungs. She's at the final stages...All we can do is to keep her comfortable. I gave her a mild sedative so she can rest through the night. I'll be back in the morning to check on your mom," concluded Dr. Fuentes.

"No! No! No!" Celia cried. "There has to be a mistake!"

Dr. Fuentes looked agonizingly at Esperanza and Legran, both mirroring his own pain. This was the worst part. These were the times he questioned his choice to become a doctor. For at moments like these, he felt utterly helpless.

For years now, tuberculosis had ranked as the number one cause of death in Puerto Rico.

Presumably responsible for the increase of the tuberculosis mortality would have been the lack of employment, which brought overcrowding in dwellings, low economic status of the island's population, and the lack of hospital facilities for the isolation of the disease were all contributing factors.

In addition, unpasteurized milk was one way tuberculosis was transmitted.

In the postwar years, state governments gradually introduced legislation to make pasteurization obligatory. Proper refrigeration of milk also helped reduce the contamination.

It would not be until years later that the first antibiotic and bacterial agent effective against tuberculosis would be discovered.

The tuberculosis mortality rate in Puerto Rico was 17 percent higher in women than in men. Pulmonary tuberculosis was responsible for 97 percent of all deaths from this disease.

The odds were stacked against Iluminada.

Esperanza went to Celia and held her tight. Celia cried until she felt completely empty of all tears. She closed her eyes and wished for sweet bliss, for surely this was all a nightmare.

Two weeks had passed since the horrible news that her mom was dying of tuberculosis. Her mom, unable to eat, had become rail thin as the disease took its toll.

Celia tried desperately to force some soup down her throat. But eventually her mother would throw up what little she was able to swallow.

Celia sat down on the bed next to her mother and stared at nothing in particular. She felt so alone. She wondered where her father was.

He left shortly after Esperanza and Legran spoke with him and explained the situation. They had even offered to help with the arrangements for the funeral, when the time came.

Her dad looked grief stricken. It wasn't until that moment that Celia realized that he did indeed love her mother. He visibly shrunk before their eyes and looked like a lost little boy. As she watched her father, Celia momentarily forgot her own pain and felt pity for him.

"Celia." Her mother's voice, barely above a whisper, brought her out of her reverie.

"Yes, Momma, I'm here"

"Sit."

At barely fifteen years old, she's losing the one person who has loved and cared for her.

"I feel it is…it is time"

"Don't! Please don't say that," Celia said desperately and squeezed her mother's hands. "You're going to be fine…"

"Listen!" shouted her mother desperately.

Celia looked at her mother. She was too startled to move, until her mother started coughing. She reached out for a handkerchief and pressed it to her mother's lips. When the coughing subsided, Celia smoothed her mother's hair back and realized her mother was burning up.

She unbuttoned her mother's pajamas and exposed her chest. She was reaching for the vapor rub when her mom caught her hand in her own.

"Celia, I have something to tell you."

"Don't talk, please, Momma."

"I have to tell you…please…"

Celia looked down, as if resigned, and waited.

"You have brought so much joy to my life, little one. I can smile through eternity because you made my life rich."

"Celia, look at me," she commanded. "You have your whole life ahead of you. Don't waste time. Please make something of yourself, and…and don't be afraid to love and be loved. You are stronger than you think. Nothing is impossible."

Celia was speechless. She wanted to be strong, but she just couldn't. She just sat there and sobbed.

She was so angry at God. Why? Why would *he* take her mother away from her? This was not fair. Not right.

Celia's vigil by her mother's side continued through the night, and sometime before the sun rose, her mother said, "I love you," and took her final breath.

At that precise moment, Celia saw something so incredible that would be embedded in her mind forever. Etched on her mother's chest…she saw a cross.

3

"**W**hy don't you just wear shit?" her father shouted. This had been the fourth time she had asked him for a new pair of shoes. He had ignored her long enough, and Celia was mad.

She had one pair that had fallen apart long ago, and tonight she confronted her dad. She refused to make him dinner, and he asked about why supper wasn't ready, she had once again asked about money for shoes.

"Very well," Celia shouted back, "then you shall *eat shit*!"

"Why, you little…ingrate! You little whore…" Her father spat and advanced toward her with a murderous look.

She had never before seen him so mad. She had been disrespectful, she knew. But the price of living with her father was too high. She had felt she needed to be loyal and stay here. She felt she needed to care for him. But looking at him coming toward her with a purposeful stride, she knew she had to leave. For living with him was not living at all.

She dashed toward the front door, but not before her father grabbed a hold of her hair. He twisted her hair around his hand and started smashing her face against the wall. But fortunately for her, he was drunk again and his balance was not quite there.

Celia managed to turn sideways and lifted her leg, praying that she would be able to land a kick anywhere on her dad's body.

And lucky for her, her kick landed directly on his left knee. In his inebriated state, her father quickly let go of her hair and dropped to the floor with a groan and a stream of explicit cuss words.

Without hesitation, she ran out the door and toward the street. She could hear her father's angry voice behind her. "Don't ever come back! You hear me? Don't ever come back!"

It had been three months since her mother had died. The whole town, it seemed, had come to the funeral.

Celia knew that they had come to bid farewell to a friend and honorary godmother to many families.

The stores in town had closed for business on this very sad day out of respect for Celia and for the love they felt for Iluminada. It was the darkest day Celia had ever experienced.

But weeks later, the constant attention from well-intended mourners left her feeling exhausted and drained.

In the past month, her five-foot frame held a body of merely eighty pounds. Her dark, rich curly black hair had become lusterless. Her big brown eyes had sunken in its sockets.

The kids at school had started calling her *bacalao*. *Bacalao* is a fish known for its unique flavor but also because it contains a lot of bones.

At first, she thought it was because she smelled, but she realized it was because she had become very skinny. Her clothes hung loose on her frame, and she had to steal one of father's belt to keep her pants and skirts up.

Although she cooked, she barely ate. It was mainly for her father that she even made the effort for.

She found it funny how her father never questioned as to where the food came from. He still remained unemployed but managed, however, to accept the monetary generosity from neighbors and friends who wanted to help them.

He never gave her any of the money for groceries or purchased any himself.

She wondered if he knew that the neighbors, feeling sorry for her, brought food and supplies over. They didn't really like her father, and she could tell by their hasty visits. Only Esperanza and Legran braved to stay longer and visit with Celia.

They had asked her father if Celia could come stay with them for a while, but her father empathetically refused. So they made it a point of keeping an eye on her.

Esperanza noticed Celia's drastic physical change but was unable to coax Celia into a regular eating schedule.

At times, Celia grew exasperated and lied to the Muñiz about eating so they would stop nagging her about her physical appearance. She didn't care. It wasn't like she would marry and have children someday. She was damaged goods.

Celia walked around town until it was almost dark. No one paid any particular attention to a boyish-looking girl with the weight of the world on her shoulders. And it was fine by her—she needed time to think.

She was too scared to go home. But even scarier was the thought of a vagabond, meaningless life. Her mother's last words played in her mind. A tear crept down her cheek. She wanted to move on and make her mother proud. She was just lost. She didn't know what or how to go about getting that dream that her mother had for her.

This was all she had known for so long.

She saw her father's rage tonight; and although he had never struck her before, she knew, without a doubt, it would be a matter of time before he'd strike her again.

And with that scary thought, she made up her mind to leave town. With shaky determination, she knew that this was her only way out of this life of misery.

She needed to pack some things for her journey. As she headed back home, she mentally compiled a list of what she would need. She had no idea where she was going. She just knew that there had to be something better out there.

As she neared her house, she noticed it was dark and she let out a sigh of relief.

It appeared her father had headed out, probably to his favorite bar. Not wanting to be spotted by the neighbors, Celia sprinted past the front of the house to the back. She hastily climbed up the backstairs and opened the back door that was always left unlocked. This door opened to the kitchen.

She walked past the kitchen and to her bedroom. Once inside, she closed the door. She looked around for a bag. Not finding one, she grabbed her schoolbag.

She emptied out the contents on the bed. She then filled the bag with as many clothes as she could fit. Everything she owned was ill fitting, but it was all she had.

She then got on her knees and pulled up a plank from the wood floor. Nestled underneath the floor was a paper sack. Celia took out the sack and reached inside for the wooden box.

The box contained three things: a handkerchief her mom had made for her for Easter, which had Celia's initial embroidered in pink on one corner; her mother's pearl necklace; and a picture of her mom that was taken when she graduated from the midwifery course.

She grabbed the box, placed the plank back on the floor, and got up. Just then she heard a noise. It sounded like whispering. Someone was in the house.

She then heard what sounded like someone clearing their throat.

She hastily grabbed her bag and put the box in it. She walked to her door and held her breath as she opened it ever so slightly. She peeked through the small opening to see if she could see who was in her house.

She didn't see anyone. All was quiet.

She opened the door a little more and stepped out.

She tiptoed past her parents' room, when she heard her father's voice, followed by laughter. It wasn't her father's laughter; it sounded softer.

Celia stood motionless for what seemed an eternity. Part of her wanted to leave and never look back. But part of her wanted to know...

She felt sick to her stomach when her feet, having acquired a mind of their own, walked toward her parents' bedroom. She put her hand on the knob and turned it ever so gently. When the door opened, the only light inside was that of the moon coming through the window.

Right there on her parents' bed, she saw her father. She wasn't quite sure for a moment what she was seeing. Her father looked deformed. There were one too many arms... one too many legs.

She then realized it wasn't just her father. There was another person, and this person was on top of him.

Celia wanted to yell, *Stop!* But she couldn't find her voice.

The other person turned around and looked at Celia. A woman.

The woman then sat up straight, and Celia's eyes dropped to the woman's bare chest, then back to the woman's face.

The woman then smiled at Celia all the while straddling her father and moving up and down.

Celia looked at her father, who had his eyes closed. He must have sensed her presence, because he suddenly opened his eyes...smiled...and slurred, "Come, say hi to your new mama..."

4

The off-duty cab driver had gone inside the minimart. Celia peered through the overgrown bush from across the street.

She saw an opportunity as she waited to see if the man would come back out quickly.

It had started to rain some time ago, and she was soaked to the bone. Having walked all night, she was exhausted. But she couldn't stop now.

Five minutes had passed and no sign of the cab driver. She decided she couldn't wait any longer and made her way to the cab.

She sprinted across the street, and within seconds, she had reached the back of the cab. She got on her hands and knees and crawled to the side of the vehicle. She pulled up the handle to the back door and said a silent, "Thank you, God," when she heard the familiar click of a door that had been left opened.

Before she opened the door all the way, she lifted her head up ever so slightly to make sure she hadn't been spotted.

No one.

So far so good.

She opened the door far enough to fit her slim frame and snuck inside the back of the cab. She gently closed the door.

She then laid her backpack down on the floor of the cab to use it as a headrest. Then she lay down, facing up.

Not a moment too soon, the cabbie came out of the minimart. He got into the car, started the engine, and started driving.

He turned on the radio, and after sifting through the limited radio stations, he settled on one that he liked. The cab filled with a melancholic tune of a man asking his woman to hate him, for hate was better than being forgotten.

Celia was startled when the cabbie began singing along, "*Odiame por piedad yo te lo pido, Odiame sin medida, ni clemencia, Odio quiero mas que indiferencia, porque el rencor, quiere menos que el olvido…*"

He had a beautiful voice, Celia thought. He almost sounded like the man on the radio. There was a soothing quality to his rendition, and she soon allowed herself to relax a bit. Knowing that her presence had gone unnoticed, she gave in to her thoughts.

Her mom had never gone into the details of sex with her.

Some things could not be spoken of. They were considered improper.

When Celia got her period, her mom taught her how to break up a towel in six parts and use the pieces of cloth to stop the flow. She learned that she had to wash each towel piece after use. She couldn't just throw it away, or else she wouldn't have any more to spare.

She never learned, however, about the process of getting pregnant. The only thing her mom ever told her was that boys just wanted one thing from a girl. And once they got it, they would lose all respect for you.

Her mom also warned about allowing boys to touch her breasts.

Iluminada always said that if boys touched her breasts, they would sag.

After this warning from her mother, Celia remembered going into her room and stripping down to her panties.

She had stood in front of a mirror and looked at her breasts from every angle. She would have never said this out loud, but her breasts could've used a little fondling.

She knew what her dad and that woman had been doing. She knew those were the things that only married people did. But no description prepared her for what she encountered.

Celia had felt betrayed. How could he do this to Momma? How could he do this to her?

Not wanting to think about her dad anymore, she closed her eyes. And within minutes, she had fallen asleep.

She had a fitful dream. She was in her parents' room. Her mom was dying all over again. Her dad stood at the foot of the bed, and he was…laughing.

Then a bare-chested woman stood out from behind him, and she too was laughing. They were pointing at her mom's dying figure and continued to laugh. Celia looked into her mother's eyes and saw emptiness and sorrow.

Celia's chest hurt. She wanted to punch her dad and that woman, but her feet were cemented to the floor. She just stood there, helpless, unable to move while the mocking laughter continued.

"I'm sorry, Momma, I'm so sorry."

5

Celia awoke with a start. She felt disoriented. She looked around and noticed she was lying in a canopy-shaped bed in an unfamiliar room.

Everything around her seemed to be engulfed in fog. There was a surreal feeling in the air.

Celia closed her eyes hard. She waited for a few minutes before opening them again. But the room was still there. She realized then that "the fog" was a mosquito net over the bed. How had she gotten there?

She looked down and noticed that she was dressed in a long-sleeved pale-blue nightgown with ruffles at the edges of the same fabric. Her feet were covered in white socks that went up to her calves.

Celia noticed a white bow on her chest. She reached for it and realized it was attached to her hair. Her hair had been part down the middle and braided in two. She reached for the second braid that had fallen behind her head and brought it forward to rest on her chest with the other.

Where was she? All she remembered was walking through the night in the rain. How cold and alone she felt. Oh, and the cab! She had snuck in the back of the cab with hopes to get out of town. She didn't even know where the cab was headed. For all she knew she was still in town, two houses away from her own house.

Gosh, how stupid could she be? What had she gotten herself into?

As if on cue, the bedroom door opened, and a pleasant-looking woman entered.

Celia was startled and sat straight up.

"Oh, marvelous, you're awake," said the woman.

As the woman came closer and lifted the mosquito net, Celia noticed she was what some called "pleasantly plump." She had shoulder-length reddish hair. Her smile was quick and comforting. Her sparkling green eyes spoke volumes of kindness. Celia decided she liked her.

"Hi, I'm Herminia," she said, "but please do call me Minnie. I always hated my name, but oh well! And, you dear, what were you thinking of? Hiding in that cab! If it weren't for ol' Gustavo, who happened to hear a noise and turned down his beloved radio, who knows? You were burning up, you see...delirious were you! Talking up a storm in your sleep. He pulled over and saw you lying back there. He tried to wake you, and that's when he noticed you were burning hot!"

Minnie didn't pause as she went on to describe how Gustavo, who was an old family friend, having no idea what to do, brought Celia to their home. Minnie and her husband Ricardo had immediately called for a doctor.

The doctor diagnosed Celia with pneumonia.

"For a while there," Minnie continued, "we were all scared because your temperature wouldn't go down. But finally, after four days, your fever broke and your breathing became somewhat normal."

"So I've been here for four days?" Celia asked incredulously.

"No, no, noooo," Minnie said as her eyes grew wide. "You've been here for almost two weeks!"

Celia, confused, stammered, "I don't understand…I thought you said…"

Minnie came closer, placing her hand on Celia's shoulder. "You've been asleep," she answered in a conspiratorial tone.

Celia's eyes grew as wide. "You mean, the entire time?"

"Yes, dear, the entire time. The doctor said you were also suffering from exhaustion and malnutrition. You poor thing! You will tell Minnie all about it, in due time. For now rest, and we will take it slowly."

She fluffed Celia's pillow and helped her lie back down.

She smoothed Celia's hair back and looked down at her kindly, then asked, "How old are you, ten? Eleven?"

"I'm fifteen," Celia responded. Feeling suddenly ashamed, she lowered her gaze.

"I take it there is no one you want us to contact? You know…to let them know you're all right…?"

Celia looked away. She bit her lip and fought back tears. "No," she replied.

"Okay, you're more than welcome to stay with us, but we'll talk tomorrow."

Minnie lowered the mosquito net, and as she was walking away, Celia said, "Minnie?"

"Yes, sweetheart?"

"My name is Celia."

6

Ponce is the second largest city of Puerto Rico. It is located east of Celia's hometown, Penuelas. The distance between cities is roughly about thirty minutes traveling by vehicle.

A couple of years ago, a peaceful march was organized by the Puerto Rican Nationalist Party to celebrate the sixty-fourth anniversary of the abolition of slavery and protest the incarceration of their leader, Dr. Pedro Albizu Campos.

The march turned into a bloody event when the insular police, a force somewhat resembling the National Guard of the typical US state and which answered to US-appointed governor Blanton Winship, opened fire upon unarmed and defenseless members of the party and bystanders.

When the shooting stopped, nineteen civilians had been killed. Over two hundred others were badly wounded. Many were shot on their backs while running away, including children who were running to a nearby church.

The US commissioned an independent investigation headed by Arthur Garfield Hays, general counsel of the American Civil Liberties Union; and in conjunction with prominent citizens of Puerto Rico, he concluded in their report that the event was a massacre, with the police acting as a mob.

They found that Winship's actions as governor were tainted with numerous abuses of civil rights.

The event has since been known as the Ponce massacre. It was the largest massacre in Puerto Rican history. As a result of this report and other charges against Winship, he was dismissed from his position and replaced as governor.

7

Herminia, "Minnie," and Ricardo Mendez saw an opportunity to make a dream come true of becoming business owners, when the Government Development Bank of Puerto Rico was created under a new generation of leaders led by Luis Munoz Marin.

The "Bank of the People," as Marin would describe it, would serve as a foundation for Puerto Rico's social and economic development.

Lacking an industrial base, the Puerto Rican government decided to take initiative and invest directly in factories that would create much-needed jobs.

So before Sears Roebuck made their presence known to the Puerto Ricans, Mendez Clothing Inc. furnished the islanders with all their clothing needs. With several chains throughout the island, the company provided evening wear and sportswear, in addition to the uniform requirements for both public and private school systems.

The Mendez ideology of fairness and good business sense made them not only the most respected couple but also the wealthiest couple. They were also selfless, compassionate, and kind. They had a deep sense of morality and integrity. If you ever saw them walking down the street, you would have never guessed as to who they were. They lacked the pretentiousness that often accompanies those fortunate to have a life with no monetary worries.

The couple, unable to have children of their own, had adopted a brother-sister pair who had become orphaned when a car accident killed both of their parents. The girl, Yolanda, had been twelve at the time of the tragedy. Her brother, Arturo, had been nine.

The Mendez had provided them with everything and more a child could wish for.

Yolanda, having finished high school, became the house manager for the Mendezes. Her duty was to interview and recruit qualified individuals to work at the Mendez home. She was also Mrs. Minnie and Sr. Ricardo's personal assistant and the only person allowed on the second floor. This is where the Mendezes had their sleeping quarters.

She was efficient and responsible but wasn't much of a conversationalist. She had no friends to speak of and only one person could ever make her smile...her brother, Arturo.

Arturo, on the other hand, was just the opposite. He was popular, charming, and witty. He delegated his responsibilities to others by promising cash, which he would later ask the Mendezes for. He was still in school, and although his grades were not a problem, it had taken a lot of influence to keep him in the exclusive private school.

He was a bright, mischievous boy, who bored easily. He had a knack for convincing others to go along with his antics and was constantly in trouble.

Mr. Ricardo would threaten punishment and give ultimatums. But he had a soft spot for the boy, and no matter what Arturo did, he could never stay angry.

Six years had passed since the adoption. The Mendezes couldn't have asked for more, that is....until Celia.

8

Sra. Minnie took Celia under her wing, and under her guidance, Celia blossomed. She was still petite, standing at only five feet tall, but her slim frame had transformed into that of a curvy young woman.

Her old clothes, no longer suitable for her changing figure, were replaced with an entirely new wardrobe.

Her hair, once lifeless, cascaded down her back with new brilliance and bounce. Celia's best feature were her almond-shaped eyes. They held a mysterious sadness that enchanted those who met her.

People were drawn to her with an irrational need to appease any anxiety that could trouble her.

But Celia's true beauty was in the fact that she was unaware of any of her attributes. She was the epitome of humbleness.

Celia had expressed her desire to finish school, and with the Mendezes's help, she not only finished but graduated at the top of her class. She was driven as if pushed by some mysterious force and wouldn't settle for anything less than perfect.

Celia had proven herself by being trustworthy, efficient, and responsible. So on her eighteenth birthday, the Mendezes made Celia the house manager, which meant Celia would not only be responsible for staffing requirements but also the personal needs of the Mendezes.

Yolanda was not happy and was quick to voice her opinion.

Sra. Minnie tried to explain to Yolanda that now she would be able to be part of managing the clothing business.

"But I have always been the one to...

"Enough, Yolanda!" Sr. Ricardo interrupted. "Our decision is final. You will teach Celia all that she needs to know." And having said that, both he and Sra. Minnie walked off.

Celia and Yolanda stood facing each other in an uncomfortable silence. Celia did not want to upset Yolanda despite the fact that Yolanda had said all but two words to her in the last three years. She had made every attempt to avoid her whenever possible. Celia did not like the feeling of taking her place as house manager and wished the Mendezes would have spoken to her first about it.

She finally dared to lift her head and look at Yolanda, and what Celia saw in her eyes was nothing short of hatred.

9

Her father, Juan Luis, had come to visit. Celia was unsure how he found her, but here he was.

He appeared sober. He had on a white shirt tucked into brown slacks. He was clean-shaven, and Celia was overpowered by the scent of his cologne.

She approached him tentatively and gave her father a quick uncomfortable hug. It was a bittersweet moment.

"You look good…," her father began. "You look like her"

"Like her?" Celia asked confused.

"Your mother," her father responded, avoiding eye contact. They stood in silence.

Her father eventually broke the silence and commented about the weather.

Celia interrupted his ramblings. "Papa, why are you here?"

Her father explained how he had sold almost everything in the house to be able to buy food. Celia had a feeling that his girlfriends did most of the damage, and all she could think of were her mother's handmade things lost forever.

She had been angry at him for so long, and now the anger had been replaced by pity. She had lost all respect for him, but she felt compelled to honor him, nonetheless.

She went inside while her father waited and fetched whatever cash she had available.

She gave it to him, and after a brief cold good-bye, he left.

He had not even said thank you.

Two weeks later, he had come back to ask for more money. Celia had refused. Her father was drunk.

He had grown outraged at the refusal and started spewing a string of cuss words. He had found some rocks on the ground and started throwing them.

Not aiming at anything in particular, yet some rocks hit the house. The noise had alerted the Mendezes, and they had called the police.

Two officers had showed up, and one of the officers had attempted to reason with her father, asking that he leave quietly. Instead of complying, Juan Luis punched the officer and soon found himself facedown, being handcuffed.

As he was being whisked away, he had looked at Celia, proceeded to spit on the ground, and wished her dead.

She did not hear from him again.

10

Something was going on.

Celia couldn't put a finger on it, but the atmosphere in the house had shifted. Sra. Minnie had been unusually curt to her, and Sr. Ricardo had not spoken to her at all.

It had been six months since the Mendezes had given her the responsibility of house manager.

Despite her personal feelings, Yolanda trained Celia. She knew that Sra. Minnie and Sr. Arturo would have held her personally responsible for Celia's success or failure in her new position.

Celia figured that Yolanda would be all business during her training but was still perplexed at Yolanda's militant-like approach. Celia needed to pay attention at all times, for there were no repetitions or multiple do-overs. She learned quickly to never interrupt Yolanda to ask questions. She had to save any and all inquiries till the end.

When the time came for Celia to prove herself, she did so and passed with flying colors. Soon she gained the trust and respect with the other household staff members. No one cared much for Yolanda, who was impervious to any type of personal hardship that may have affected the staff at any given point in time.

Celia, on the other hand, had been a godsend to the hardworking staff who oftentimes had to either leave their young children with neighbors or relatives or trust the child home alone while the parent worked.

Celia understood this all too well, having been that child at one time who took care of herself while her mother worked and her dad stayed out drinking.

Celia was fair and kind. And when an emergency arose with any of the staff's family members, Celia would make adjustments to scheduling to accommodate the employee. And if need be, she would take on a task to cover for the employee until they were able to come back to work.

This selfless demeanor rallied the staff with a sense of teamwork and loyalty toward Celia.

So with the palpable change, Celia could not figure out what was wrong. She had not done anything out of the ordinary; but it hurt, nonetheless, that if she had indeed done something, she would have been spoken to accordingly and be given a chance to redeem herself.

Celia was overseeing the supper menu when Lupita, one of the younger maids, came into the kitchen to tell her that a man was asking to speak to her and that he was waiting in the living room.

Celia looked at Lupita and frowned. The question unspoken.

Lupita shrugged and said, "I don't know who it is, Senorita Celia. It's a man with a huge mostacho. Never seen him before."

Celia nodded and made her way into the living room.

The man stood up and walked toward her with his hand outstretched.

"Salvador Morelli," he said.

Celia shook his hand and almost smiled at the sight of the man's mustache. Lupita had not been lying. His mustache was an exaggeration on his bony-like facial structure.

"Celia," she said in turn.

Celia immediately noticed his eyes. They were very dark and predatory like. She noticed how they quickly scanned her from head to toe, and she was positive he had taken in every detail of what she was wearing.

His intensity had unnerved her. She wondered who he was and what he wanted with her.

Salvador Morelli reached into the pocket of his cream-colored guayabera shirt and pulled out a cigarette and a box of matches. He then lit the cigarette before Celia could protest.

He then took a deep drag, exhaled the offensive smoke toward Celia while never taking his eyes off her.

"Please sit down," he said as he gestured to a chair and proceeded to sit across from her.

"Umm, Mr. Morelli," Celia began, "there is no smoking in the house. If you prefer, we can speak outside on the terrace?"

Mr. Morelli didn't respond immediately. He stared at Celia and proceeded to take another puff of the cigarette and exhale. Then another puff...

Celia was about to stand up and gesture for him to follow her to the terrace, when he swiftly put the cigarette out by pinching the tip with his thumb and index fingers. He then placed the unused portion back in his pocket.

Celia gave an inward sigh of relief.

Mr. Morelli cleared his throat. "I am a detective, and I have been hired by Sr. Ricardo because someone in this house has stolen a certain amount of money from the Mendezes."

Celia looked incredulously and asked, "What do you need from me?"

"Just some simple questions I need answered. I shouldn't take much of your time," he replied.

He proceeded to asked Celia what was the nature of her relationship with the Mendezes and in what capacity she helped the Mendezes. He asked for a complete description of her job duties in addition to any incidents that may have deviated from a normal schedule.

Mr. Morelli inquired about the second floor and who had access to that level of the house.

Celia responded quickly and spared no detail. She had nothing to hide, although she had a suspicion that the detective knew the answers to all the questions he was asking her.

He asked about a particular day earlier in the week. Celia knew the schedule by heart as she had been the one to put it together. It was laundry day.

Mr. Morelli asked what took place on this day, and Celia explained the process from beginning to end. It appeared simple on the surface, but everything had its place, and every item had to be handled in the most conservative of ways to preserve the fabrics.

"Did anything out of the ordinary or unusual happen on this day?" he continued.

Celia was quiet for a moment, trying to recall if anything out of the ordinary had happened.

"Any detail that may seem unimportant or irrelevant at the time…?" Mr. Morelli pressed.

"Well…"—Celia remembered—"Señora Minnie and Señor Ricardo asked me to fetch them some towels. They were at the pool, you see, and had forgotten to get some beforehand."

"So did you fetch them their towels?" Morelli asked.

"Well, yes…I mean, no," Celia stammered.

"Well…what was it, Celia? Yes or no?" he asked, confused.

Celia took a deep breath and became suddenly nervous. "Well, I was on my way up, but I saw Yolanda coming down, and I asked her if she would please fetch the towels for me," she finally said. "I wouldn't have asked her, but I was in the middle of training a new employee."

"And did she fetch them for you?" asked the detective.

"Yes," Celia answered.

The detective's face was unreadable as he concluded the interview. "If I have other questions, I know where to find you."

Celia walked Mr. Morelli to the front door.

He turned, shook Celia's hand once more, and walked out.

As Celia watched Mr. Morelli walk away, she felt the familiar fear that had threatened to consume her so long ago when her mother was dying. The fear of abandonment. The Mendezes had become like her parents. Although no one could ever take the place of her mother in her heart, Sra. Minnie filled in the void that was left when her mother passed away. Sr. Ricardo was everything her father wasn't. He was supportive and caring. He made her feel protected.

Did they feel the same way about her, or had she been a charity case? Did the Mendezes believe she had stolen the money? Is that why they had been distant with her?

So many questions…

She had no reason to steal. The Mendezes had been good to her. Plus, her mother's words resonated in her head still. "Never let your name be known for a couple of dollars."

One thing she knew for sure, regardless of the outcome of this investigation, things would never be the same.

11

The cloud of suspicion hung heavy over all in the house in the weeks to come.

The Mendezes remained cold and distant. Mr. Ricardo spoke to her once and that was to advise that until further notice, the second floor would no longer be part of her responsibilities as head house manager.

Celia continued the rest of her duties as house manager. With the extra time, she turned an empty storage room into a child care room.

She wasn't sure how long the ban for the second floor of the house would remain into effect, so instead of the continued worry that plagued her, she would put her energy into something useful and meaningful.

The staff had become her extended family. As much as she poured into them, they poured into her. Their loyalty gave her purpose and hope.

The new room would allow for those employees without extended families or trusted friends to bring their children and be cared for while their parents were at work.

The new girl—Amelia, whom she had been training some weeks ago—proved to be perfect to oversee the task of the child care center.

Amelia and Celia put together a roster to keep track of the children, in addition to a schedule of activities and meal plans.

Celia had some reservations about the success of the child care center. She wasn't going to be able to help Amelia full-time, and she feared that this project would be a bust without the extra help.

She walked into the center one day to check on how things were going and noticed that the room had been divided into groups. She saw each group had a teen or preteen either reading, telling stories, or playing games with the younger children.

She looked at Amelia and asked, "Did you put this together?"

"Yes…," Amelia answered hesitantly.

An idea came to Celia in that instant. "Amelia, you are a genius!" she said as she reached for a shocked Amelia and gave her a tight warm hug.

Celia explained to Amelia that she would "hire" the teens to help out in exchange for an allowance. Celia would have to withdraw the money from her own salary to pay the teens, as she did not wish to approach the Mendezes at this time with the request.

Once everything was settled and things hopefully returned to normal, she would approach the Mendezes about it. In the meantime, she would handle this.

12

A knock on her door startled her.

Celia opened the door to find Yolanda.

"Mr. Morelli is back. He wants us all to gather in the living room."

When she and Yolanda entered the room, the only other people there were Sra. Minnie, Sr. Ricardo, and Arturo.

This couldn't be good, she thought.

Everyone was seated except for Mr. Morelli, who was standing in the middle of the room. The room had one large sofa and two smaller chairs. Sra. Minnie and Sr. Ricardo were on the sofa. Arturo was half sitting on the armrest of one the chairs. Yolanda sat on the chair with her brother, Arturo, leaving Celia the remaining chair.

No other persons were in attendance, which meant that either Mr. Morelli was going to speak with the family first and tell us what happened to the missing money or the culprit was amongst the five of us. And seeing that the

Mendezes were the one who called the detective, who only left Yolanda, Arturo, and her.

"I asked you all here," Mr. Morelli began, "because I have solved the case of the missing money."

"Well, tell us! Tell us who dare disrespect us and steal from us!" Sr. Ricardo exclaimed.

"Before I do, Mr. Mendez, I would like to take a moment to fill you in on how I reached my conclusions."

"Very well then, make it quick," Sr. Ricardo added with a disgusted face.

"One singular bill worth one hundred dollars needs to be broken down not only for fast spending. Because in the event of ever being questioned, the perpetrator would not have the incriminating bill in their possession."

Wow...one hundred dollars! Celia thought. Up until that moment, Celia had no clue how much money had been stolen.

Salvador Morelli paused, as if for dramatic effect, and then looked at each one of us. He then continued, "I checked all local markets, convenience stores, gasoline stations, and such until I happened upon an establishment that, as luck would have it, the owner remembers the customer paying with a hundred-dollar bill. He remembers the transaction because someone sporting that kind of money was not an everyday occurrence.

"The owner stated that the customer spent twenty-three dollars and fifty-two cents for a variety of items. He was kind enough to compile a list of the purchased items. I have the list here, if Mr. Mendez cares to see it?" Mr. Morelli said, reaching into his pocket.

"But as of right now," he continued, "I'm taking the chance that no more money has been spent and this person should have in their possession exactly seventy-six dollars and forty eight cents."

"Okay, Morelli, enough drama. Who took it?" Sr. Ricardo asked, clearly containing his temper.

Mr. Morelli put his head down and took a deep breath, then turned slowly around and said, "Arturo?"

Arturo jumped up. "Are you crazy, man? I don't have to show you anything! Some detective you are. You are so wrong…"

Until that moment, Celia had not realized that she had been holding her breath. She looked over at the Mendezes.

Sr. Ricardo was looking at Arturo with unbelieving eyes. Sra. Minnie was crying quietly.

Celia looked over to Yolanda, but she had her head down.

Mr. Mendez slowly got up and walked toward Arturo. "You don't believe this? Do you, Papa?" Arturo asked.

"Show me your wallet, son," Sr. Ricardo asked.

"But, Papa…," pleaded Arturo.

"I said, show me your wallet! I will not ask again!" shouted Sr. Ricardo, startling everyone in the room.

Arturo looked over at Yolanda. As if sensing her brother's look, she looked up and nodded. Arturo took out his wallet and handed it over to Sr. Ricardo.

Ricardo, with much deliberation, opened the wallet and found a picture of Sheila, the girl next door; a business card with the Mendez logo; and, to his dismay…seventy-six dollars and twenty-three cents.

A slight miscalculation somewhere, but enough proof as to who the culprit was.

"I'm sor…," began Arturo. But before he could finish, Sr. Ricardo slapped him across the face.

Arturo held his cheek and looked at Sr. Ricardo in shock. He had never been smacked before.

"I…do not allow thieves under my roof! Pack your bags. I want you gone by morning," Sr. Ricardo said with a low, menacing voice that sent shivers down Celia's spine.

Then Sr. Ricardo walked over to Yolanda. "You knew all along, didn't you?"

Yolanda just looked down and never answered.

Mr. Morelli quietly let himself out.

Sr. Ricardo walked out of the living room, and a few seconds later, a loud slam was heard. Sr. Ricardo had locked himself in his study.

Arturo went to go pack. Yolanda followed Arturo.

Sra. Minnie stayed seated right where she had been and continued to cry. Celia wanted to comfort her. The sight of Sr. Minnie in tears tugged at Celia's heart. But she had not felt the courage to approach her, so she quietly got up and went back to her room.

13

Celia was incredibly sad and heartbroken. She was not close to Yolanda, but Arturo had never done anything to her. He was always charming and funny whenever he saw her.

With false determination, but knowing it was time, she found the set of suitcases the Mendezes had given to her for her birthday last year.

She placed them on the bed, opened the first one, and, with a heavy sigh, started packing.

She was so completely concentrated on her task that she had not seen Sr. Minnie standing in her room until she had asked, "What are you doing, Celia?"

"I think it's time for me to leave," Celia answered, not stopping her task.

"But where…why…? Oh, Celia," Sra. Minnie asked in an agonized tone. "What a mess this has been!"

Celia continued packing.

"I want you to know that I never thought you were the one. I suspected Arturo from the beginning." Minnie had come to Celia's room to apologize for the indifference of the past week, but she soon realized that Celia's pride had been at stake—especially when she had been innocent.

So instead of trying to stop her from leaving, which she knew would prove futile, she decided to help Celia pack.

Celia understood a mother's love. She really did. The need to protect their young and still Celia could not comprehend how a person can go from being a trusted and loved member of a family to being made to feel as if she had done something wrong.

She had felt confused and lonely. These feelings were part of her life so long ago, and she naively thought they had been left in the past when she found the Mendezes.

But this was not the only reason she had felt the need to leave. She was eighteen years old, and she wanted more.

She looked up from her task, and Sra. Minnie was still standing in her room. She had a worried expression, and she was wringing her hands nervously.

Celia loved this woman. She had been like a mother to her when Celia was left broken by her mother's passing and her father's noncaring demeanor.

She walked to Sr. Minnie, and the two women embraced. They then sat at the foot of the bed and talked for hours.

Celia told Sr. Minnie she had heard on the radio about a need for immigrants to work in the United States. The airfare was free. The only documents required from those who applied were a birth and health certificate and an eighth-grade diploma.

Celia explained to Minnie that this seemed to be a good opportunity, and she wanted to pursue the possibilities of a life outside of Puerto Rico.

Minnie was a tad apprehensive and told Celia as much. She promised to make a few calls to make sure this venture wasn't a ploy to lure unsuspecting young woman for God knows what means.

Minnie looked at Celia with a mixture of love and sorrow. "Are you sure that I can't change your mind about staying?" she finally asked hopefully.

Celia looked at Sra. Minnie and saw the kindness in her eyes that had greeted her in this very room three years ago. She had known that she was breaking Sra. Minnie's heart. It was the last thing she had ever wanted to do. But as difficult as this was going to be, she had known this was the right thing for her to do.

"I'm sorry...," was all Celia could respond before she broke down and cried softly.

Minnie embraced her. "It's all going to be all right. I'll be here for you always, my Celia. This will always be your home."

14

The next day, Minnie made a few calls to check into the immigrant program. She spent all morning taking notes and covering every detail.

Once satisfied that the program was not a hoax, she helped Celia fill application and get the documents that were needed to qualify.

Since the Mendezes had a good standing in the community, Celia was able to have her application reviewed and approved in two days' record time.

Ricardo had not spoken to Celia since the incident with the missing money. He didn't understand why he hesitated to speak with her. He attributed the hesitancy with feelings of guilt. He too had felt that Arturo had been the culprit, but for once he had wanted to be wrong about his gut feeling.

He could never kick his son out of his home. He had been angry and disappointed. But after he calmed down enough, he spoke with Arturo.

The boy had cried and had asked for forgiveness. Ricardo promptly forgave and had asked what had been so important that he had felt the need to steal the money instead of simply asking for it, as he had in the past.

Arturo had confessed about giving cash to this girl Alicia, and in exchange for the cash, she would show him her breasts. Alicia was a classmate of Arturo. He first learned about what she did through his friend Joaquin.

After school, Joaquin had taken Arturo to Alicia's house. He had given Arturo twenty-five cents for him to give to Alicia when it was his turn to go into her bedroom. Arturo stated he had been nervous but wanted to see what she looked like anyway.

He told Sr. Ricardo how he had felt guilty for what he had done and confessed to his sister, Yolanda. He said that Yolanda had told him to not worry and they discussed how she would help him tell their parents the truth.

When Mr. Morelli was hired, both he and Yolanda had become too afraid to say anything, so they kept quiet.

Ricardo had listened intently to Arturo. He felt he had missed a crucial step about his son's education. Sex or sexual urges were not topics that were openly discussed. He had been a young boy when he learned a few things by eavesdropping on his father and his friends during domino night. He had been caught hiding under the table; and instead of his dad giving him a good licking with the belt, he had sat him down, looked him square in the eye, and told him he would allow him to stay but that this was a man's night and that the girls were not allowed to know what they did or discussed.

Ricardo remembered feeling like a grown-up. He loved his father for making him feel as a trusted member of the "man's club" as his dad had referred to it. The men never discussed their wives.

Ricardo had learned early on that this was a sign of respect for their partners and mothers of their children. They only brought up each other's spouses when speaking of who had cooked what delicious meal. They did, however, discuss the "loose women" who lived around town and what they've heard from other guys about what these women did.

Up until this moment, it had never occurred to Ricardo that his son, much like himself at this age, had been curious. He did not condone the stealing or the lying, and he made sure that Arturo understood that he could always come to his father regardless of what it was. He then had made a mental note to speak with Yolanda. He loved his daughter. She was bright, articulate, and extremely reserved. The pain of losing her birth parents and feeling responsible for her younger brother could not have been an easy journey to overcome…if she had ever.

Yolanda was very protective of Arturo, and although she knew that he and Minnie loved them, at times he wondered if her heart had closed for good on any other love other than her brothers.

Ricardo found Celia in the child care center. He watched with awe and pride as she spoke with Amelia about changes in the schedule as some of the older kids were leaving to go to college soon.

Minnie had already discussed with him the funding for the child care center, and they jointly decided that this had been a great idea, and why had they not thought about it early on? This simple step made the staff happier and eager to be working in a place they felt valued.

Celia had a great sense of people and business. He knew she would be successful in whatever she decided to do with her life.

Ricardo hated the thought of her leaving to a foreign country all by herself. His mind drifted back to when he had first seen her. His old friend Gustavo had her in his arms. She had been soaking wet and delirious. She looked so small and malnourished, and he remembered immediately mentally cussing the parents of this poor girl.

He and Gustavo would speak extensively during the days to come in the hopes of figuring out who she was and what was her story.

It wasn't long before they were able to piece bits of information together and had a clear picture of who Celia was, her mother's death, and her father's reputation and neglect of Celia. As a man of honor, he had sent word to her father of Celia's whereabouts.

Following her father's conduct when he visited the house last, Ricardo had made a silent vow to protect Celia.

And now, here she was. A beautiful and intelligent grown woman.

Much like with Arturo, Ricardo felt he had failed her. And although he was not the drunken, abusive man her father was, he was far worse. He knowingly and willingly made her feel like a pariah these past weeks.

She didn't deserve that, and if anything, she needed to know that he was sorry.

Celia looked up from the schedule sheet to find Sr. Ricardo looking at her with a pained expression. She excused herself with Amelia and approached Sr. Ricardo.

"Are you all right?" Celia asked concerned.

Ricardo gave a quick nod. "May I speak with you privately, Celia?"

"Sure," Celia responded and followed Sr. Ricardo to the garden on the east side of the house. The flowers were in full bloom as the hummingbirds danced their way from one flower to another. Sometime last year, a small waterfall was built on the far end of the wall. The water led to a small pond came the home of a variety of different-colored fish. On the other end of the garden was a gazebo. This was Celia's favorite part of the garden. She had spent many an afternoon here reading some of her favorite books.

Knowing this was Celia's favorite place, Ricardo walked over to the gazebo and encouraged Celia to take a seat.

Celia had never seen Sr. Ricardo so nervous before. He was always calm and reassuring. She waited patiently as Sr. Ricardo took a deep breath.

"Celia," he began, "I know I have wronged you, and you did not deserve that."

75

Celia shook her head no and was about to protest, but Sr. Ricardo made a motion with his hand to allow him to continue speaking.

"All I've ever wanted for you from the moment you arrived was for you to feel safe, loved, and protected. And now you are leaving because of this whole ordeal…"

"Sr. Ricardo," she dared to interrupt, "I'm not leaving on account of anything that has taken place here. The only thing that this experience has managed to do was give me perhaps the incentive to live my own life. I want to explore, learn, and venture out of the island…"

Celia wouldn't tell Sr. Ricardo this or anyone for that matter, but she had felt limited with the Mendezes. She was grateful for their help and always would be, but she did not want to feel as if her life had been handed to her on a silver platter. She wanted to pave her way and for once feel the satisfaction of actually earning something.

She wanted to be courted by men whom she would deem worthy of her affection and not have handpicked suitors "accidentally" being paraded in front of her or conveniently being introduced to her at one of the many parties the Mendezes would go to. She couldn't explain it. She would never begrudge anyone for their financial status, but she wanted a man who knew the value of hard work and earning his keep. Not a man lucky enough to have parents, or even grandparents, who had worked for their success and in turn their offspring would be guaranteed a job in the company without ever having earned it. These men would never know the struggle of finding a job, keeping the job, and supplementing the needs of their family.

Celia knew she was generalizing. She had indeed met an individual who did not fit into that category. His name was Ismael. His father was in banking, and his mother was an actress. She had met Ismael at a charity event. No one had introduced him. They had bumped into each other at the buffet table.

They hit it off immediately. They exchanged life stories, and he confessed to her that when he was finished with college, he was leaving to the States to pursue a career as a writer. His parents knew and were disappointed that he was not going into the banking business. They had had several arguments with him, but he would not be made to feel guilty for living his life.

Sparks did not fly between Ismael and Celia. It so happened that Ismael liked boys, not girls. Celia did not understand this concept but did not judge Ismael and kept his secret. She knew this concept was not very well received by Puerto Ricans whose Catholic teachings and beliefs were very stringent and unyielding at the time. Maybe in the United States, Ismael would find others like him and be able to have a family of his own as well. He had been a good friend, and she would definitely miss him when she leaves.

Celia looked at Sr. Ricardo and saw the love that she would have seen in her own father's eyes. Whereas Minnie had been *like* a mother to her, Sr. Ricardo *was* the father she never had. It was painful to see him torturing himself over something that was done and in the past. "Sr. Ricardo, I can't forgive you, because there is nothing to forgive. I have felt safe and protected. I have felt loved. There is nothing more I could've asked for."

Sr. Ricardo had reached for Celia and had hugged her tight. "I am so proud of you, *'mija. Dios te bendiga y los anjeles te protejan siempre.*" May God bless you and angels be with you always. He then had kissed her forehead and went back inside the house.

Celia was touched. For a fraction of a second while in Sr. Ricardo's embrace, she had felt as if she was making a huge mistake. What was she thinking leaving the home and the family she had grown to love?

But wheels were in motion, and now ready or not, it was too late.

15

The staff had thrown her a small good-bye party the night before her flight. Even her friend Ismael had been there. There had been tears free flowing, but Amelia had been a wreck. Celia had become like a big sister to her.

They staff had all pitched in and had given Celia a gift.

Celia had unwrapped the present to find a box. Inside the box been a gold necklace that held an oval-shaped medal with a picture of the Virgin Mary of the Sacred Heart. The vivid colors and the image were exquisite.

Celia had been touched and moved to tears. Ismael had come over to hug her. "She will safeguard you during your journey, *mi amiga.*"

After the party had ended and being forced to leave and not help with the cleanup, Celia had gone into her room to finish the last details for her flight in the morning.

Although she didn't need anything, Sra. Minnie had taken her shopping and, in addition, had given her cash to use in case of an emergency. Celia had saved most of her salary and attempted to refuse Sra. Minnie's offering, but her protests fell on deaf ears.

She changed into her pajamas and got ready for bed. She had a long journey ahead of her, but she was too nervous to sleep.

She looked around her room. She remembered waking up in here for the first time. It's seemed like yesterday and yet so long ago. She had felt lost, afraid, and devoid of all hope.

She was different now.

The Mendezes had helped her see her potential, and she will be forever grateful.

Her thoughts shifted, and she dared to think about her mother. She had not thought about her in a long time. Thinking about her brought a sense of loss and melancholy. But tonight she wanted to think of a happy moment.

She thought of one of her mother's stories of delivering the baby of a coworker from the fabric store. The coworker had been told she would never be able to conceive. She and her husband had tried unsuccessfully for years to have a baby.

Mom had said the woman had no idea that she was pregnant. She told mom that she thought she was getting fat because she was eating a lot of fried foods.

During the day, she had complained to their boss that she was not feeling well. Short time later, Mom was on her knees, delivering a baby. It had been a healthy baby girl.

"All you need is a little bit of faith," she had told Celia that night. That was the one thing her mother always would tell her.

And with a hopeful smile, Celia had soon fallen asleep.

16

The Mendezes drove Celia to the airport.

Saying good-bye to them was one of the hardest things she had ever had to do. They were people whom God had placed in her path to help nourish her soul, regain her inner strength, and allow her to see her path in life.

They had given her guidance and a new sense of worth that had been misplaced when her mother died. As long as she lived, she would never forget them.

Soon Celia was aboard a cargo plane. She is one of the twenty-two young women who had been chosen for the immigration project.

Celia had never flown before. She realized she had been afraid. She wasn't sure if it had been the thought of being above ground or the fact that she was in an enclosed area with so many people.

Soon the plane made its way on the runway and took off. Celia's stomach had been in knots since before the departure. Despite the warning, Celia had still been unprepared for the amount of turbulence that took place.

Soon, she found herself unable to breathe, and she had been fighting waves of nausea for what had seemed an eternity.

The young woman sitting next to her had realized what was going on with Celia. "Come, put your head down in between your legs," she said, holding Celia's hand.

Celia obeyed.

"That's it....breathe deeply...in...out...in...out. Don't think of anything except of me holding your hand," she said.

Celia soon felt better. The young woman had gotten up against the advisement of the flight staff and promptly had returned with a wet washcloth. She then placed it on Celia's neck, and it had felt wonderful!

When the nausea had subsided, Celia looked over at her savior. She looked like an angel. She had the blondest hair Celia had ever seen. Her eyes were the blue of the ocean. She was the most gorgeous creature Celia had ever laid eyes upon.

The girl was smiling. "Hi, I'm Ursula."

She smiled back and responded, "I'm Celia."

Soon the young women were exchanging their life stories, and there was a sense of ease about their exchange. It's like they had been lifelong friends.

And before too long, they had arrive, both feeling excited and apprehensive of the new life that awaited them.

17

Chicago, USA, 1944

The letter said,

> *Ursula,*
>> *Please help me, Celia*

Celia was being held against her will in the home of Pricilla and Milton James.

She worked for them as a servant. This seems more a befitting word than *maid*. The Jameses treated her like an animal. No...much worse.

At first glance, they were the all-American dream couple. They were what some might call "old money."

Priscilla's great-grandfather, proving his business savvy at a young age, owned the first import-export business of livestock. Milton's family, on the other hand, were in banking.

The marriage of Priscilla and Milton was a business venture that proved fruitful for both families. And generations to come will benefit from a life of luxury.

The Jameses hosted a number of charity events throughout the year that benefited a number of organizations. They had been major sponsors in the recruitment of young immigrants under the guise of giving minorities an opportunity for a better life.

They were very much respected.

But the public image of philanthropy was nothing but a ruse. Because behind closed doors never existed a worse set of bigots. To say, they had contempt for Hispanics was an understatement. They believed that Celia was beneath them.

This treatment of contempt was all too familiar for many of the girls who had made the journey with Celia.

Sometimes the man of the house, making sure not to leave any visible marks on the girl's body, would whip them with a belt.

But regardless of treatment, they stayed. It was scarier to be proven weak and return home a failure. So they suffered in silence under the hands of prejudice.

The dream was not just theirs anymore. It was the dream of their mothers and fathers. Brothers and sisters left behind. The dream was too big to give up.

Celia was constantly humiliated and ridiculed because her English was not perfect. What little did she know she learned from school and listening to her surroundings.

Her employers knew she had no family, so they took advantage of her. They kept her locked up, so she wouldn't take her days off. And ultimately, she didn't get paid at all.

One night, after a surprise visit from Milton, whose intentions with Celia were less than honorable judging by his lascivious stare, Celia had made it a point of locking her door.

She had been able to fight him off, and he eventually had given up…that night.

Soon after, it became a nightly ritual. Obviously drunk, he would come to her door and shout for her to open the door when he discovered it to be locked. She had even pushed her dresser in front of the door for extra security measures.

But last night had been different.

Celia had finished up the last of her chores and headed toward her room up on the third floor. She had been contemplating a nice hot shower when she entered her room and was greeted by both Priscilla and Milton.

"Milton tells me we have a problem," Priscilla said.

"I don understan wat yu meen?" Celia responded.

Priscilla walked toward Celia and touched her hair. "You see, Celia, if my husband is unhappy, then I'm unhappy. I thought perhaps you needed some motivation…" She gingerly touched Celia's arm, then slowly moved her hand up and cupped Celia's breast.

Celia smacked Priscilla's hand away and turned around. She bumped into Milton, who grabbed her by the waist and began licking her neck. Celia could hear Priscilla in the background, "Don't fight us, Celia. You will find out it's a waste of time. You belong to us now, and the sooner you realize that, the better."

This could not be happening to her.

She had managed to get loose from Milton and bolted to the door, only to find Priscilla blocking her way.

She was trapped.

She started walking backward to get as much distance as she could from them—her eyes never leaving their faces. She knew she was outnumbered, but nonetheless she was going to fight them with all she had.

Then the doorbell rang.

"Shit!" mumbled Milton.

Milton and Priscilla stood still. Waiting.

The doorbell rang again.

"Shit! Shit!" Milton said again.

He left the room to see who was at the door.

Celia was alone with Priscilla.

She was contemplating ramming into her and making a run for the door, but Milton came back. "We have a problem at the warehouse," he told Priscilla, obviously not happy at the turn of events.

"Please do wait up, Celia. We have unfinished business," purred Priscilla.

And they left—but not before bolting Celia's door from the outside.

Celia ran to her window and looked out to make sure their car was actually headed out the driveway. A while back she had tried to escape through the window, but there was a lead bar across it. When pushed, the window would open slightly but not wide enough for a child to push through, let alone a grown person. All she had managed to get out the window was her hand, and that almost got stuck at the wrist.

She paced her bedroom. "Think, think," she urged herself.

She had to get word to Ursula. But how?

She rummaged through her drawer and found a scrap of paper. She hastily wrote the note and sealed it in an envelope. She knew the address by heart, having written to her almost weekly—that is until the Jameses prohibited any outside communication for fear that Celia would report them.

Celia and Ursula, having bonded during their journey to the States, remained close. They were makeshift sisters, supporting one another and trying to find their way in a foreign place.

Because the immigration program was a one-year contractual agreement, the women had the same schedule. They worked for their sponsored families (employers) five days a week and had the weekends off.

The goal was for the women to become financially independent, integrate, and become part of a community until they were completely independent at contract's end.

The women took their time off to go sightseeing and learn more about the culture. They learned of a small Catholic church where the priest spoke Spanish, and during their first visit, they met other women who had made the same journey as them months prior.

At first, all appeared to be going as planned.

Ursula and Celia swapped stories about their employers. Ursula's employers had been extremely kind to her. They went out of their way to show their appreciation of her. Celia did not dislike her employers; there was just something about their smiles that never reached their eyes. It had made Celia uneasy.

Ursula had told her she was being paranoid, but still Celia could not relax.

At first it had started with the Jameses advising Celia that she needed to work Saturday. Scared to say anything contradictory, she complied.

She told Ursula the next day on their way to church. Ursula told her that maybe it was "one-off" and things should be back to normal soon. To not worry.

Two weeks later, it happened again.

Not happy with the situation, Celia requested to know why she was needed. Priscilla had lashed at Celia and told her she was not to question their decision, and as punishment for her insubordination, the Jameses withheld her Sunday too.

Weeks to follow the nightmare continued and escalated. From no days off, withholding her pay, cutting off any outside communication to the sexual advances.

And now, as she looked out of the barred window, she wondered how she was going to get out of this predicament.

She closed her eyes and said a silent prayer as a tear rolled down her cheek.

When she opened her eyes, she saw a gentleman pass by down the street below. Seeing an opportunity, she pushed her hand through the narrow opening of the window, and with a quick wrist movement, she threw her letter out.

As the letter floated in midair, Celia yelled, "Hey! Hey! Look up! Psst!" But she was unable to get the gentleman's attention.

The letter continued its descent, but by the time it hit the ground, the gentleman had already walked on by.

For some strange reason, as Celia watched defeated, the gentleman had turned around.

He stopped when he saw the letter on the pavement. He picked it up and looked around. He looked at the letter again and turned it over, as if looking for a return address.

Celia tried to signal him, waving her one hand frantically through the barred windows, but he never looked up.

He then put the letter inside his coat and walked away.

Celia watched the streets below for a long time, but he never came back her way.

All she could do now was wait.

Book II
Nando

1

Guayanilla, Puerto Rico, 1934

"Man! What's that stench?" Pedro asked out loud.

All the kids in the classroom started looking around for the cause of such disgusting odor. It was a mix of fish in a hearty broth of clogged-up sewage.

"Class, let's pay attention now," Mrs. Gutierrez said.

"But, Teacher, it really stinks back here, more than ever!" Pedro replied.

A collective of "*ay fuchilas*" and "pews" were followed from the rest of the kids.

"Okay, okay, I'll see what I can do. In the meantime, here is your corrected test from Monday. As some of you will soon find out, the results of your test were not very good. To these students, I will be speaking to you and your parents sometime this week."

Before he had a chance to view his test, Nando knew that he had failed. Actually he was failing in every class. He knew he would have to repeat the grade. This didn't bother him. School was a waste of time. At least for him it was. He knew he wasn't particularly intelligent. He had already gotten used to the snickers and comments from the other kids who called him names.

As Mrs. Gutierrez approached his desk, Nando fidgeted in his seat. He was, to say the least, very shy. He expected the outcome of his test; but, nonetheless, for one brief moment, he dared to hope that it would be different this time. Hoping made him nervous...he hated this feeling, and so he looked down.

Mrs. Gutierrez placed his test on his desk, and he took a glimpse. There it was...an F—a nice, big red bold letter that was as plain as a pimple on someone's nose.

The teacher made a tapping sound on the desk as to get Nando's attention. At the precise moment he looked up, he could see the painful realization in her face.

She knew.

Her eyes had watered, and she was speechless. She looked down at his feet and noticed his shoes. If you could call them that. There were barely covering his toes. They had broken apart months ago.

What was once white now seemed to be the color of baby poo, and he had no laces either.

Nando was embarrassed. He couldn't take it. The shame had caught up with him. And as if possessed by a demon, he got up and ran.

He ran out the door, past the courtyard, to the streets.

He could hear his teacher calling for him. But he kept running until he couldn't hear her anymore, until he couldn't hear anything anymore. Just the sound of his own heart that threatened to jump out of his chest.

Without realizing it, he had come to the river. In the past, he had enjoyed the solitude and beauty that the river provided. It was as if anything that was wrong in his world seemed unimportant here. But today, not even the calming waters could contain his frustration. He sat on a rock and wept.

He looked at his feet and saw the source of his shame. In one swift movement, he took off those retched shoes and flung them into the air. They fell somewhere in a tree. He didn't care, for he rather walk barefoot than torture himself with the daily reminder that he was unloved.

Nando had asked his mother, Juana, when they would be able to go shopping. She always responded, "Soon." She would send him to do chores, and when he was done, he was surprised to realize that his mom had taken his sister shopping instead.

It became such a routine that he eventually stopped asking, for he knew that he would never go anywhere with his mom.

He wondered why she hated him so. Why was she ashamed?

Nando had eyes the color of a thunderous sky and hair that was considered "good," judging by what he overheard his sister's friends say. He didn't know what that meant, but he figured it to be a compliment.

His skin was the color of an old penny, and he often wondered if this was why his mother hated him. This seemed ironic to him because he looked exactly like her.

His sister, on the other hand, had creamy white skin, blue eyes, and long straight blond hair. She favored their dad.

His dad, Salustiano, was a good man. Everyone in town adored him. He always went out of his way to help others.

His mom and dad had opened a small convenience store adjacent to their house. Two years ago, Hurricane San Ciprian had destroyed the little establishment and part of the main house as well.

His parents rebuilt the little store as an attachment to the main house. So instead of going outside to get to the store, all you had to do was cross a hallway from the living room to a side entrance of the store.

They sold things like chips and candy. His parents had chickens, so they sold eggs as well. Bakery-type bread, goat milk, colas, and of course who could forget the beer?

People from the neighborhood would drop by the store and just stay talking to his dad. They were never in a hurry to leave. Pretty soon, the sidewalk in front of their house became sort of a meeting place where sports, politics, and the latest on "who was doing what" were exchanged.

The store was the sole argument his parents had had for years. For his father would stack up groceries for the needy and make rounds around town. His mother highly disapproved. For she felt it wasn't good business to be giving things away. She thought one should profit at another's expense and profit highly.

He loved his dad. But his dad was weak. He never interceded when Momma got out of hand. It was as though he had been afraid of her.

His sister, on the other hand, wasn't afraid of anything. She was younger than he. But what Momma's attention might have made for a spoiled child, his sister was completely selfless. She always stuck up for him with Momma. And when Momma was in her moods and took to beating Nando, his sister always comforted—always told him that things would get better.

He knew, without a shadow of a doubt, that he would gladly give his life for her. She was the only thing that brightened his day. The only thing that had any meaning in his life.

2

On her way home, Mrs. Gutierrez thought about Nando. He was a quiet kid, who kept to himself. He was very respectful, and he had never been a problem student.

Teachers would never admit to having a favorite student. Those are for the most part the ones that participate and do well in school. It made the teachers feel respected when a student paid attention, participated, and in turn received good grades.

But for Mrs. Gutierrez, being a teacher was about reaching those children who appeared unreachable, the ones who came to school and attempted to blend in with their own shadows.

Prior to today, she had tried to reach out to Nando to help out with his homework. He had shaken his head no, turned crimson red, and had run off.

During recess, she always witnessed Nando going off on his own with a book. He would sit in the same shaded spot under one of the trees and read until it was time to come in. This made her wonder as to why he was failing academically. Reading is learning. So what was she missing to connect it all together for him?

Having an idea, the following day, she had waited until he had sat down under the tree. She had walked over to him and sat down beside him.

Nando barely looked up.

"What are you reading?" she had asked.

Nando simply closed the book so Mrs. Gutierrez could see the title, *El Grito de Lares*. Mrs. Gutierrez knew the story well. It was a classic in Puerto Rico's rich history.

"Would you like to tell me what it's about?" she pressed gently.

Nando shrugged.

They sat in silence.

Not wanting to make him more uncomfortable, Mrs. Gutierrez was about to stand up and leave, when Nando finally said, "It's about a small revolt that Puerto Ricans had planned to protest the Spanish rule on the island."

Mrs. Gutierrez nodded her head to encourage Nando to continue.

Visibly relaxing, Nando had explained how a Puerto Rican socialist named Ramon Emeterio Betances, who was an advocate for the island's autonomy from Spain and who had been exiled twice for his political views, planned an armed rebellion with the pro-independence movement.

Betances had been frustrated by the lack of political and economic freedom, which brought about more repression on the island. He also condemned Spain's unwillingness to abolish slavery.

Mrs. Gutierrez watched Nando's expression as he continued explaining the story. She had never before seen this side of him. She had completely misread him.

He was highly intelligent and insightful. It was clear based on his appearance that he was failing for lack of care and guidance.

She had not realized that Nando had finished speaking and had been looking at her with questioning eyes.

She collected her thoughts and said, "I'm glad you shared this with me."

Nando had turned red again and looked back to his book. By then recess was over, and the two walked side by side back to the classroom.

The memory of that day brought her to tears.

How can a child be so neglected? He was a good child and deserved a chance.

Mrs. Gutierrez felt bile rise in her throat as the image of his shamed face looked up at her today, and then she had known what she needed to do.

3

The cockroaches climbed all over the wall around him. They were as big as the palm of his hand—so big in fact that he could see their heads turning and their eyes looking at him.

He was locked up in the outhouse.

He came home from the river, only to find out that his teacher had visited. His mom now knew he cut class and was failing.

She was outraged; and after punching him in the face and kicking him several times, she grabbed him by the shirt, dragged him through the room and down the cement steps, and locked him in here.

He couldn't figure out why was she mad. It's not like she cared about him. Maybe she was upset at being embarrassed by what he had done.

What seemed like hours had passed. He had managed to concentrate on a small opening in the wall to avoid thinking of the fluttering and hissing of the roaches. They came out of the latrine in groups. Nando stood in a corner, painfully trying not to have any part of his body touch the walls or the latrine.

It was getting darker outside. He was getting scared. With each passing minute, he feared he had been forgotten.

His stomach made a growling sound. He had been fighting the feeling of nausea for the last hour. He was getting dizzy. His legs were about to give out on him. How long had he been standing still?

His clothes were sticking to him. It was unbelievably scorching hot. Droplets of sweat poured from his forehead, and he wiped furiously, thinking that the roaches were crawling on his face.

He could hear the crickets and the "coquis" outside. Coquis were the miniature frogs that lived on the island. A rooster sang in the distance, announcing the end of another day.

He then heard a rustling sound. Someone was outside, or so he thought. Maybe his mind was playing tricks on him, yet he listened intently, but no other sound came.

Then there was a thump, a click, and the door flew opened…It was his sister.

"I'm so sorry. I had to wait until Mama went to bed," she said.

"That's okay," he said and hugged his sister.

"Listen, Nando, I think you should leave, ya know? I love Mama, Nando. I really do, but…I hate that she does this to you…" She cried as she hugged her older brother tight.

"I thought about it, but I can't leave you here. Plus, where would I go?" Nando asked.

His sister thought for a second. "What about your friend Guillermo? I'm sure his mom wouldn't mind if you stayed with them if she knew what was going on here? And as for me, don't worry. I'll be fine. You just don't deserve this."

"Yeah, well, I guess I'm not as pretty as you," Nando responded with a dry laugh.

"Stop it. Don't say things like that," she protested and playfully punched her brother on his chest. "You're going to make us all proud someday."

"I seriously doubt it. I have no hopes of finishing school. I'm not as bright as you are. No one will ever take me seriously. And, furthermore, I…"

His sister once again protested and interrupted her brother's sentence. "I said stop that nonsense talk!"

Nando watched his sister speak animatedly about a beautiful future—one that was only possible in the dreams she had for him. He listened with a sad smile and wished for once he could take away some of her hope for something good to happen to him.

She startled him when she jumped up as if the devil was pulling on legs. "Oh! Ah! Before I forget! Come here!"

He followed his sister to the bushes behind the outhouse. She seemed to be looking for something.

He was about to ask what was she looking for, when he heard her say, "There it is!"

She handed him a box.

"What's this?" he asked

"Open it," she commanded.

Inside the box was a brand-new pair of black shoes. They had laces and were shiny. Right beside it was an envelope.

"What in the…?"

"Just read the note, Nando!"

He handed the box back to his sister while he read the note. It said,

> Nando,
>
> I'm sorry about today. I hope these fit you. Please come back to class. I can help you.
>
> Mrs. Gutierrez.

"I don't understand…," said Nando. He was shocked, touched, bewildered.

"When your teacher came over today, she was telling Mama about what happened at school. She was saying that she could help you pass the grade. Mama interrupted her and told her that you wouldn't be going back to school. That you were old enough to work. Mrs. Gutierrez told Mama that was a mistake. She said you needed school. Mama was outraged and told Mrs. Gutierrez that she would make any decisions she well pleases. Then she told her that she had to leave. I was listening to the whole thing from the back door, and when your teacher was leaving the house, I followed her outside.

"Then what happened?" Nando asked in amazement. He had never heard of anyone speaking back to his mother—that is, if they wanted to live.

"Well, I caught up with her and started to apologize for Mama, but Mrs. Gutierrez stopped me midsentence and told me to give you the box. She said something about how she now understands and it was she who was sorry. She made me promise again to give you the box. I had to go through the back of the house so Mama wouldn't see," she said in a hushed voice.

"Wow." It was all Nando could say. No one had ever gone through so much trouble for him before.

"So what are you going to do?" his sister asked.

"I don't know," he replied. "I just don't know. The first thing, though, for now, I would like to eat. I'm starving!"

His sister nudged him with her elbow, and they both giggled.

"And you need a shower too!" she chided.

"Yeah, yeah," Nando replied. And they giggled some more.

Nando placed Mrs. Gutierrez letter back into the box. Before covering the box, he looked at the pair of shoes one more time, and for the first time, he knew what hope felt like. The gray cloud that forever loomed over his head seemed to have dissipated somewhat.

It wasn't the shoes, he thought. It was the thought that someone other than his sister had shown that he was worthy of love.

Nando and his sister walked hand in hand back to the house.

"Oh, and by the way, Nando, happy birthday," she said.

Nando stopped and looked at his sister.

He had completely forgotten that today he had turned thirteen.

4

"*Maldito! Desgraciado!*" His face was being pressed up against his own vomit.

His mom had her knees firmly wedged in his back and a firm grip on his hair.

It was getting harder for him to breathe.

He felt like passing out a couple of times but, instead, closed his eyes and prayed that his mother's rage would be over soon. She had become upset because the floor had just been mopped and he had not made it to the "puke" pail on time.

He had contracted some sort of virus. The results were fever, diarrhea, and severe stomach cramping. He had thrown up until he dry heaved. But his mom refused to get the doctor. She said he was a man and thus needed to be tough.

Unbeknownst to Nando, his sister, having grown increasingly worried, had gone to get help.

She couldn't think of anyone else but of Guillermo and his mom, Elsa.

They had become aware of Nando's situation at home some time ago and had been outraged. They readily had offered him a place to stay; but Nando, not wanting to leave his sister, had refused.

Nothing prepared Elsa for what she witnessed as she entered Nando's home.

"Stop it, Juana!" Elsa yelled.

Guillermo tried to pull Nando's mother off him. But Juana was strong and determined, and she elbowed Guillermo in the ribs.

Elsa also tried to get Juana off Nando but was rewarded with a punch in the face.

"This is none of your concern!" Momma yelled, "This is my son, and I can do with him what I please!"

Nando could hear his sister crying and screaming for Momma to let him go. It was a surreal moment.

Then in the midst of all the chaos, Nando heard a thunderous voice that shook him to the core, for he had never heard this voice before. At least not this way.

The voice only said one word, "Juana!"

Everyone stopped to see who had spoken. It was his father.

Juana looked at Salustiano and—having never seen the murderous look before on her husband, Salustiano—decided it was best to not chance further confrontation. She then slowly got up.

Salustiano looked at Elsa and ordered, "Take him with you now!"

Juana stood quietly as Elsa and Guillermo whisked Nando away. And not wanting to waste any time, they had decided to take him straight to the hospital.

The doctor had confirmed that Nando had a stomach virus, but other than severe dehydration, he would be fine in no time at all.

Antibiotics and various intravenous fluids had been quickly administered. He was also given a weird-tasting medicine to stop the dry heaving.

Nando stayed in the hospital for a week. But there was never a dull moment since Guillermo, Elsa, and his sister frequently visited him.

Together they would sit around and laugh at Guillermo's descriptive narrative. He was a born comic and always kept Nando laughing until his side hurt. Guillermo could imitate anyone he wanted to.

Elsa would stay later on some nights and read stories to Nando. It made him feel like a kid again.

Mrs. Gutierrez had stopped by once to see how Nando was doing and to encourage him to continue school. Nando agreed to think about it but knew in his heart that he would never return. School just wasn't for him.

On his third day, his father came to see him.

Nando had just finished a hearty breakfast of watery unsalted eggs, hard toast, prunes, and skim milk. He had been thinking that if the virus didn't kill him, the food surely would, when he looked up and saw his father standing by the door.

His father was smiling uncomfortably. He had taken his hat off and was wringing it in his hands. A sure sign that he was also nervous.

The room had gone silent as father and son just looked at each other. Then slowly, his father made his way to his son's bedside and, with a tear-stricken face, embraced him.

In his father's arms for the first time, Nando let his own tears flow freely. His father had then kissed the top of his forehead and quietly left.

He never said a word.

Nando sat there pensively. He wondered how two people could be so opposite and still be together. Love was funny that way he guessed.

He knew his dad loved his mom, for he had seen the look on his dad's face when his mother had entered a room. She had been completely oblivious of the reaction she caused for his dad or the depth of his feelings for her.

Nando heard one time that his parents' marriage had been an arranged one. His grandparents on both sides were said to be wealthy. He had never met his grandparents from either side.

He wondered if they still lived—not that it really mattered at this point.

Then he thought of how he couldn't bring himself to hate his father for just allowing things to happen for so many years. People just are who they are, and he had learned to accept the fact that his dad was a passive man who detested confrontation.

He would never understand what had prompted his father to stand up to his mother that night, but he knew that he would be forever grateful for the chance at a normal life.

He felt hopeful for the first time in his short life. His friends had bestowed him with more attention, love, and care than he had ever dreamed of.

When the time came for him to leave the hospital, with a clean bill of health, Elsa and Guillermo had asked him to go live with them.

This time, he didn't hesitate at all and said yes.

With Guillermo's help, Elsa had fixed up a spare bedroom for Nando, and when Nando saw his new living quarters, he wept.

5

It had been four years since Nando had come to live with Elsa and Guillermo. They had become his family.

Guillermo's dad left when he was still a baby. Elsa had become both mother and father for her young son. She never remarried, so she bore all the economical responsibility.

She had rented a small one-bedroom house and had been forced to find jobs that would be lenient to accept the fact that by hiring her they would have to deal with her bringing Guillermo along.

Some of the employers didn't mind on account of Elsa being a hard worker. On occasion, she had been lucky enough to have employers hire extra help to assist with Guillermo.

But some other employers would eventually make unwanted sexual advances toward Elsa.

Elsa rejected them all. She had long ago determined that her dignity and self-respect were not for sale.

If the rejection didn't get her fired on the spot, ultimately, when the wives found out about their husbands infatuation with Elsa, she would find herself jobless.

These unfortunate situations occurred more times than she desired, and when faced with the predicament of either paying rent or putting food on the table, she eventually became homeless.

She sought refuge at a local Catholic church. The nuns, taking pity on Elsa and Guillermo, offered them a place to stay.

Although it was communicated to Elsa that she was welcomed to stay as long as she needed, pretty soon she realized she was overstaying her welcome.

A chance encounter with an elderly woman named Belinda at the minimart would change the course of her life.

The woman, having struck a conversation with Elsa, was moved by the girl's candid manner and offered her a job and a place to stay.

Belinda had no children of her own and was immediately taken with Guillermo. She offered to care for him while Elsa worked.

The "work," as it turned out, was to be a companion of sorts to Belinda. She was growing in age, and although her mind was sharp and her heart was willing, her joints had been slowly deteriorating by arthritis. Daily routines had become quite an effort.

The arrangement suited both women well. And in years to come, they would become more than employer and employee; they would become friends.

When Belinda died, she left the house and all her possessions to Elsa and Guillermo.

She had also left Elsa a moderate sum of money that, if used wisely, would last Elsa for years to come.

6

"You wanna touch it," Maritza said as she spread her legs open even farther.

Nando had just stepped out of the shower to find her stark naked on his bed. He was shocked.

Maritza was his next-door neighbor. She was nineteen, and he had a crush on her since he first laid eyes on her, six months ago. She and her family had just moved in.

Her dad, Sr. Julian, had come over to introduce himself and asked if he knew of anyone who could help him paint the outside of his home. Nando and Guillermo had volunteered.

When Nando saw Maritza for the first time, he thought he was having a heart attack. Her skin was the color of freshly brewed coffee with a hint of milk...and maybe a spoonful of sugar. She had long jet-black hair that went down past her back. Nando had never seen so many eyelashes on the most amazing darkest set of eyes.

So for two weeks straight, while Guillermo and Nando painted, Maritza would sit in the balcony and chat with them. Actually she chatted with Guillermo as he was the talker, and Nando would just listen since he was the shy quiet one.

So now, looking at a naked Maritza, he wondered for a second if he was dreaming.

"Maritza, what are you doing?" he asked when he finally found his voice, which sounded like a dying frog.

"Whatever do you mean?" she replied seductively. "I just thought it was time you should be with a woman."

Maritza batted her eyelashes and licked her lips. She cocked her head to one side and said, "You haven't been with a woman yet, have you?"

Nando felt "things" happening to his body, and much to his embarrassment, Maritza also noticed these "things" happening to his body when he saw her looking toward the bulge in his pants.

Maritza gestured with her index finger for Nando to come closer. Nando was transfixed and walked mindlessly to his bed where Maritza was in all her womanly glory.

He sat beside her. She was so beautiful, and she was right in front of him, naked.

Maritza took Nando's hand and placed it in between her legs. He was not sure what he was supposed to do. All he could feel was an enormous amount of hair. He mentally imagined walking through a jungle in search of a hidden treasure. The image almost made him laugh, but he was sure it would have hurt Maritza's feelings.

She guided his hand to a certain spot, and by her sudden intake of breath, he knew he was on the right track. He leaned in and kissed her.

And the rest was a blur.

7

He had woken up naked.

At first he had been disoriented, wondering why he had been naked. Then he remembered...Maritza.

It could have been a dream, except it had not been because...well...he was naked. He smiled.

He could still smell her scent on his pillow.

Maritza had been his first, but he was certain that he had not been her first. He didn't care. He was in love.

He and Maritza would get together almost every night after that. They would take turns sneaking into each other's homes. He couldn't get enough of her.

Maritza had found in Nando an avid student and a gentle lover. He was patient and considerate.

On some nights, Nando and Maritza would lie side by side and talk until they would hear the roosters announcing the dawn of a brand-new day.

They talked about their dreams and their lives up until that point. Maritza had cried when Nando spoke about his mother and what his life had been like four years ago. It had been the first time he had spoken about his parents to anyone outside of Guillermo and Elsa.

Elsa had figured out that Maritza and Nando were seeing one another.

She had confronted Nando. "Do you love her?"

"Yes," Nando responded proudly.

"Then you need to do the right thing. You need to talk to her father, Nando."

Nando knew that Elsa was right. He knew he was young still and had nothing much to offer Maritza, but he did want to marry her.

He had walked to the river and had sat on his favorite rock. He had rehearsed what he would say to her father, and it had all sounded extremely dumb. What was he going to say? "'Sr. Julian, I love your daughter, sir. I want to marry her, and we will live in a cardboard box'?"

Nando practiced some more. "Sr. Julian, I love your daughter, and I don't have a lot of money now, but I would like your permission to marry your daughter...eventually... before I die of stupidity."

Maybe if he wrote Sr. Julian a letter? "Ahhhh," he had yelled, exasperated.

Nando had decided that he would just have to say what needed to be said regardless of how it all sounded.

With a determined stride, he made his way to Maritza's home.

He had never spoken to Maritza about marriage, but his heart knew that she loved him too.

He was about to reach her home, when he heard her voice.

"Nando!" He looked across the road to see Maritza coming from the direction of his home. "I was just looking for you."

Nando met her halfway and could tell instantly that something was wrong. He could feel the knot forming in the pit of his stomach.

"What's going on?" he asked with concern when he reached her.

Maritza fidgeted for a moment and did not give Nando any eye contact. When she finally looked at him, no words were needed to be said after a young man dressed in a military uniform walked toward them and put his arm around Maritza. "There you are!" he said.

The man looked over at Nando. He smiled as he extended his hand to introduce himself, "Hello, I'm Jaime. Maritza's husband."

Nando had felt his face flush.

He shook Jaime's hand. "Nando," he managed to say, and with one last look at Maritza… he walked away.

8

For a couple of years now, Nando worked on and off doing odd jobs for the neighbors. Painting, carpentry, cement mixing. Since he was honest and very hardworking, word had spread like wildflower of his attributes. Pretty soon, friends of his neighbors called for him, then friends of the friends.

He had bought a few things for himself with the money he had earned, but most of it he gave to Elsa to buy food and other things that were needed. At first she didn't accept the money he had offered but grew tired of arguing with Nando.

He just felt it was his duty to contribute.

He never saw Maritza since that faithful day years ago. He had heard from Guillermo that she had moved to the States with her husband; and her parents, having learned that Maritza was expecting her first child, eventually moved to the States as well to be close to her.

He had hurt for a long time.

His quiet demeanor as he grew older gave him an aura of mystery. His body had turned lean and athletic on account of the physicality of his various jobs. But his best feature were his hazel eyes. The contrast of those eyes against his skin always made women do a double take.

Nando didn't have to try very hard. Women pursued him, and he allowed himself to be seduced…over and over again. None of these encounters lasted more than the one night…or day, much to the women's disappointment.

He learned soon enough that all women were different. They smelled different and tasted different too. He treated every single one as if they were unique and beautiful, and they all loved him for it, but Nando wasn't truly invested in any of them.

One day while sitting at the breakfast table sipping his coffee, Guillermo joined him.

"Hey, did you hear the news?" Guillermo asked.

"What news?" Nando replied distracted.

"Well, it seems they're asking for young women to work in the States"

"What do you mean? To work doing what?" Nando asked suspicious.

"As maids is my guess"

"Maids! *Hijole*! Go figure!" said Nando, completely disgusted. "What do they think, these Americans, that we can't do anything else except clean toilets?"

"It's a chance to have a better life, Nando," Guillermo reasoned.

"A better life! Cleaning toilets?"

"Well, I'm pretty sure the girls won't be doing that all day."

"Yeah, I bet," Nando said and sipped his coffee

"Well, I wish I were a girl because I want to go. I'm tired of working my ass off for a measly pay," said Guillermo.

"And to think *you* finished school." Nando laughed.

"See that's what I'm saying. I know I can do something different. I know it would be so much better in the States."

"Well…if you really want to, I can help you."

"Help me how?" asked Guillermo, suddenly alert.

"I can buy you a dress, get my sister to do your makeup, and with that *culito* you got going on back there, we can get you outta here!" Nando said, laughing.

"*Ay so maricon!*" Guillermo said, laughing too, and punched Nando.

Nando puckered his lips and pretended he was blowing a kiss to Guillermo.

In between his laughter, Guillermo said, "Ay, Nandito, you know you want me."

"Sure, *mamacita*," responded Nando.

They were laughing hysterically just like when they were kids. It felt good.

Their laughter was interrupted when Elsa walked into the kitchen.

"I have cancer," she said.

9

They stood under the rain, watching the casket being lowered into the ground.

The dirt under their feet had turned to mud on account of the unforgiving weather.

Nando and Guillermo stood side by side and silently wept. Rain and tears mixing together, both tasting the same.

It was inconceivable to them that only one year ago, Elsa had told them she was dying.

Elsa had explained that the malignant tumor had spread to all her vital organs. It was only a matter of time. When she was done explaining all that she knew about her illness, Guillermo had run out of the house. He had been beyond despair.

Elsa knew her son and knew that he just needed time to think and be alone.

Nando had just sat and stared at his hands.

Guillermo had come back by dinnertime. Nando and Elsa could tell he had been crying.

As they all sat around the table, it was, with silent understanding that the subject of Elsa's cancer would not be discussed. At least not that night.

Guillermo, as only he could do, began telling some outlandish story about a random goat and a chicken. Pretty soon they were all laughing and telling stories until dawn.

The months and days leading to Elsa's death were perhaps some of the most painful and trying days Nando had experienced. He felt for his friend, his brother. Elsa was all he had.

Guillermo never knew his dad, nor did he care to. Elsa had done a fine job being both mother and father to him.

Elsa had been that for him too.

Nando will never forget the day Elsa and Guillermo took him away from his home and his mother's abuse. She cared for him as if he was her own son.

She had filled in the void and healed his soul. He would've been lost for sure. He owed her everything.

Watching her suffer and in pain was unbearable.

Nando and Guillermo were by her side when she made them promise to watch out for one another and be good men.

She expressed regret for not being around for when they would fall in love, get married, and have children.

They all cried and held hands. And sometime during the night, she was gone.

She was suffering no more.

And now, here they were, saying good-bye to a wonderful woman. It wasn't fair, Nando thought, that the most evil people get to stick around and live to make others miserable, while the good-hearted ones are taken too soon.

Nando and Guillermo headed back to the house, as it was customary for the mourners to visit after the burial. Neither one was up for the task of entertaining, but decided the faster they came, the faster they would leave.

Hot cocoa was passed around. Cheese, salami, and crackers were offered.

When the last of the mourners left, Guillermo and Nando sat in the balcony.

Neither one spoke for a long time. Each lost in their own thoughts.

Nando broke the silence. "Remember that talk we had about leaving Puerto Rico? Are you still wanting to leave?" he asked.

"Oh yeah, nothing here for me. Except the house. I can try to sell it, but that can take a while. I may just close it up in case things don't work out, you know. Why?"

"Well, I was thinking that if you still wanted to go, I would go with you," Nando replied.

"You would?" asked Guillermo incredulously.

"Of course, you're my brother. What did you think? I would let you leave by yourself? Plus, my sister's application was accepted for that maid deal you had told me about."

"I didn't know she had applied!"

"Yeah! So you see, nothing is keeping me here either," Nando said.

Guillermo looked down and said, "Thanks, brother. But if we're gonna do this, we have to plan."

And so they planned.

10

Nando and Guillermo kept coming back to the same problem: money.

They had some money but not enough to buy a plane ticket and have funds to live on for a couple of weeks until they could find jobs in the States.

Whatever little money Elsa had, had gone into her funeral expenses.

Selling the house would take some time. They decided they would rent it out but struggled to find a trustworthy individual to oversee that the property was cared for and funds were collected appropriately.

While on a paint job for a local business, Nando overheard some of the other men who were hired were discussing the influx of tourists who were coming into town. Apparently, two cruise ships had docked by the port not far from where he lived.

He then had a crazy idea and couldn't wait to tell Guillermo.

"*Estas loco?*" exclaimed Guillermo when Nando proposed the idea.

"Porque? Why? Do you have any better ideas? We have been going over this for months!" Nando responded, exasperated.

"But there has to be something else we are not considering," reasoned Guillermo.

Nando had proposed that the two travel to the States as stowaways on one of the cruise ships.

It was risky, but it was worth the try.

"Quite frankly, Guillermo, I'm ready to leave," said Nando, defeated. "With Elsa gone and my sister living her new life, what is keeping us here?"

Guillermo thought about it for a minute. He knew Nando was right, and really neither of them felt they had anything keeping them here. There was nothing to lose.

"Okay, Nando, let's do it," Guillermo finally said.

In the weeks to come, they both will walk around the docks and keep track of the staff and their routine. There were different supply trucks that came in daily. At least two staff members from the ship would meet up with the trucks at the dock.

On more than one occasion, they noticed a young boy coming out from the ship and meeting up with the supply trucks. He will then run back up the plank and back into the ship. Soon after, Nando and Guillermo would see the same two staff members come out. The men will then unload the truck and bring its contents into the ships through the lower level.

They saw a plan forming when they saw the boy leave the ship and head toward the beach. They watch him as he collected seashells. He could not have been more than ten years old. Perhaps twelve tops.

Nando decided that Guillermo should befriend the boy as he was more personable.

Nando would hang back within listening distance.

And so Guillermo approached the boy and introduced himself. The boy's name was Antonio, and his father was the head chef on one of the ships. His family lived in Florida. He was the oldest of three children, and he was twelve years old.

The boy warmed up to Guillermo immediately, just as Nando predicted.

Soon he could hear the boy laughing at Guillermo's jokes, and after talking for a while, Antonio said he had to go back to the ship before they come looking for him. He promised to meet up with Guillermo the next day.

The next day, Antonio came back to the beach.

Guillermo and Nando were already there. He introduced Nando to Antonio.

The boy had looked at Nando and wasn't sure what to make of him at first but, seeing his kind eyes, decided Nando was okay. Antonio's mother always told him that "the eyes were the windows to the soul."

Antonio told them that this was their last night on the island. Nando and Guillermo looked at each other and knew they had to take the chance.

So with absolute remorse and attempting to appeal to the boy's sympathy, Guillermo told the boy about his mother, Elsa, and not having any family left—that they needed to sneak on the ship because they had no money.

"Who will meet you in the States once you get there?" Antonio asked.

"No one," responded Guillermo.

"I have a sister," Nando said. "We will find her."

Antonio looked down at the sand in between his toes. He picked up a seashell and placed it in his pocket.

Silence stretched as Antonio struggled with the decision to help them. He could get in trouble, but maybe it wouldn't be too much since his dad had an important position on the ship.

"Okay, I'll help you."

They were to meet up within the hour. That's when the guards changed shifts.

Nando and Guillermo didn't really have enough time to pack a whole lot of things. So they grabbed some essentials, locked up the house, and headed toward the dock to wait for Antonio.

They feared he had changed his mind as minutes passed and no sign of him.

Then they saw him. He was running toward them.

"Sorry, I had to eat dinner. Come on! We don't have much time," Antonio urged.

With ten extra dollars in his pocket, which he initially refused, Antonio would lead Nando and Guillermo to a hiding place aboard the ship.

The hiding place was a storage room that was barely used. Antonio promised to check in on them as much as he could.

And if all went well…they wouldn't be discovered.

11

Galveston, Texas, 1943

They had been in jail for five days.

They were discovered in Guantanamo, Cuba, immediately handcuffed and placed in a small holding cell aboard the ship with a security guard on watch.

They had kept them in restraints until the ship docked in Galveston.

Antonio had been bringing them food and water. His father, growing suspicious of the possibility of a thief amongst the personnel, hid in the kitchen.

Imagine his surprise to find his own son filling a sack with food. Upon confrontation, the son led him to Nando and Guillermo.

"I'm sorry, Papa, but I had to help them." Antonio cried.

The father, feeling no sympathy, immediately turned them in.

Upon their arrival in Texas, the immigration department had been called. The department investigated both Nando and Guillermo and, not finding any history of felonies for either of them, concluded that it would be a waste of time to send them back to Puerto Rico.

Nando and Guillermo were relieved.

The Red Cross aided in their release from jail—and provided them with food and warm clothing. They found a fleabag motel where they would stay for the time being until they could afford something better.

For weeks, Nando and Guillermo searched for employment. Sometimes they got lucky and managed to get temp jobs for minimal pay. These jobs were usually unloading or loading boxes or cases of a variety of things such as books, electronics, fruits, or vegetables.

But overall, these jobs would inevitably end, and the time unemployed grew longer and longer. Soon, what little money they had ran out.

With no place to go, they would sleep in shelters and eat when they could. If shelters were full or closed, they would depend on the kindness of strangers along the way. They went from city to city. It was all the same.

Until one day, quite by accident, they went their separate ways.

They had reached another city. One like so many others. All the while hoping that this city would be *it*.

But *it* was not meant to be. At least not here. At least not yet.

It was getting late, and by the time they reached the shelter, it was closed.

They decided to head to the nearest train station. They would get on the next train and stay on it until the last stop.

This would give them some rest time and decide what their next move should be.

When they reached the station, the next train had already arrived and was about to close its doors. Nando and Guillermo ran to catch the train.

Nando was faster and made it before the doors closed.

As the train picked up speed, Guillermo ran alongside it, and with one last look at Nando, he waved good-bye.

12

As the train rocked him back and forth, Nando had been lost in thought. It had been two weeks since he last saw Guillermo.

He missed his friend…his brother.

He figured at some point he needed to become an independent man. But at this point, he was too tired to even try.

He fell into despair. No one would give him a chance. Wasn't this supposed to be the land of opportunity?

He missed his sister too. Last he heard, she was living with a rich couple and was reassured that she was being treated well.

He wanted to see her, but in his present condition, it wouldn't have been a good idea. It was inconceivable for him to disrupt her life with the troubles of a vagabond brother. It was not fair.

"*Hablas espanol?*" the man across from him asked.

Nando looked around to see whom the man was talking to. It was to him.

"*Si*," he answered.

"*Que bien*," the man responded. "My name is Esteban. But people call me Paco."

"Mine is Nando."

"Where you from, Nando?" Paco asked.

"Puerto Rico," Nando responded.

"*No me digas*! You don't say! Me too. What city?"

Nando was unsure if he should say the part where he lived with Guillermo and Elsa or the part where his parents lived. He opted for the latter. "Guayanilla," he finally responded.

"Say! Me too! Funny how we never ran in to each other?" Paco said enthusiastically. Then he added, much to Nando's surprise, "Did you live close to Salustiano's convenience store?"

Too stunned, Nando replied with a simple, "Yes."

"Did you know the owner died last week? My mom wrote to me and told me. She said it was the largest funeral in the history of Guayanilla. That man was very loved and respected, you know. He would've taken the shirt off his back to give to anyone in need. When he found out I was leaving town, he gave me some money and wished me well. I'm not sure, but I know they had a daughter. She was a beauty. My mom said they had a son too, but I never..."

Nando had tuned him out. He felt dizzy.

His father had died, and he didn't even know it.

He should've gone to see him when he had the chance. Oh God! How many times had he tried to summon the courage to go?

"Hey! Are you all right?" Paco asked.

Nando simply nodded.

"Anyway, um, I don't mean any disrespect, but, um…do you have a place to stay?"

Nando looked down at his filthy clothing. He caught a reflection of his unshaven face on the train's window. He had not realized he had looked so bad.

He looked over at Paco and needing to just talk to someone and share his burdens, he decided to tell him what had happened.

By the time the train had reached its next stop, Paco had a clear picture of Nando's circumstances and compelled to help his newfound friend, Paco offered Nando a place to stay.

Nando readily accepted.

Paco worked as a cook at a local restaurant and told Nando that they were hiring an extra cook. So the very next day, wearing the only suit that Paco owned, Nando interviewed for the position.

Nando was immediately liked and offered the job.

Proving to be a fast learner, within weeks, he quickly moved up to the position of assistant chef.

Things were starting to look up for Nando.

The extra money had allowed him to eventually move out of Paco's place and rent an apartment of his own.

His new living quarters were modest but more than enough for him and his measly possessions.

He hadn't bought any furniture, save for the bed. But he did purchase a car. He never owned a car before, and for the first time in his life, he was feeling proud of himself.

But he was alone. Having no one to share his day with had washed him in feelings of melancholy.

He missed his sister. He missed Guillermo.

He missed not ever having an actual girlfriend. Not having the love of a woman, actual love.

Nando's skin had lightened a bit since he came to the States. He had let his moustache grow. It went well with his full head of hair. He thought it made him look more sophisticated.

He still maintained his toned physique, and standing at six foot and two inches tall, he hardly ever went unnoticed.

The women whom he worked with at the restaurant had commented that he had "tornado" eyes. They gave the impression that there was a "whirlwind" of mixed emotions passing through him. He was always teased about how people could always tell what mood he was in just by looking at the color of his eyes.

When he was disturbed or preoccupied, they favored green. When he was in good spirits, they were a light grayish blue.

Nando, by all means, always exuded mystery. He was still quiet and always the hard worker. Very seldom did he volunteer any information about himself.

And although he thought some of the women he met were gorgeous, none captured his interest, much to the women's dismay.

Feeling a bit nostalgic, he decided to write to his mother. He had no idea what he would say.

He wrote several drafts that ended in the wastebasket. Nothing seemed appropriate.

The he decided to just make it quick and simple.

He gave a brief description about his newfound life. He inquired about his sister and her whereabouts. He inquired about the store. With his father gone, he wondered if she had decided to keep it open. He added that he hoped she would write soon.

And before sealing the envelope, not wanting to send just the letter, he had also enclosed a twenty-dollar bill. He felt a misplaced sense of duty. He was still her son, and no matter what, that couldn't be changed.

He sent off the letter and hoped for an acknowledgment.

The response came three and a half weeks later.

His heart was beating fast, and he broke out in a sweat as he fumbled to open the letter.

Still, after all this time, his mother had an effect on him.

His mother had been very brief.

> *Nando:*
> *Your sister is alone. Be a man and go to her.*

Enclosed with her note were two things: a piece of paper with his sister's address and his twenty-dollar bill.

Book III
At Last

1

She heard Ursula calling out her name.

Celia had fallen asleep and woke up with a start at the frantic calling of her name.

She yelled out, "I'm in here."

She heard a loud crash and then running. "Celia! Celia! Answer me!" Ursula urged.

"Upstairs! I'm upstairs," Celia yelled even louder.

She heard voices, then jumbled words, and she pressed her ear to the door.

Ursula was not alone.

"I'm in here!" she repeated.

They were outside her room.

She heard a click, a thud, and then the door swung open. Ursula's sweet face came into view, and she ran to Celia, and the women embraced.

"We've got to hurry! Your *patrones* should be back soon!" Ursula rushed Celia.

"Wait, I need to get my things."

Celia packed as quickly as she could, but she couldn't find her box—the only keepsake she carried everywhere.

"*Apurate*, Celia! Hurry up!" said Ursula impatiently.

"Looking for this?" Stunned, they turned around to see Milton holding Celia's box. Celia, darling, are you going somewhere?" Milton said, and then he looked at Ursula and said, "You, my friend, are trespassing."

The women looked at each other. Ursula grabbed Celia's hand and squeezed. This was her way of telling Celia that they were in this mess together.

With renewed strength, Celia cleared her throat and said, "I'm leaving!"

Milton laughed. "Leave! You can't leave. You have a contract, my dear. Or have you forgotten?"

Celia never missed a beat. "I don't care! I'm not staying here a minute longer!"

Milton's face became a purple-reddish color.

"Why, you little piece of…" But before he could finish, Ursula's companion, who until now had gone unnoticed by Celia, punched Milton smooth in the face and knocked him out cold.

For the first time, Celia looked at the man who hit Milton.

He had retrieved Celia's box from where it had landed on the floor when Milton fell. He then walked up to a speechless Celia and said, "I believe this belongs to you."

Celia took the box and managed to say, "*Gracias*."

Ursula hastily grabbed Celia's bags and handed them to her companion.

She then looked at her friend. "Celia, I'd like for you to meet my brother, Nando."

2

Celia was sure they would encounter Priscilla on their way out, but their hasty departure went without further incident.

Nando's small car waited for the trio downstairs, and he drove straight to his and Ursula's apartment.

Ursula explained to Celia that when Nando arrived, with his excellent references, he quickly found a job at another restaurant.

She then told her employers that she would continue to work for them but was going to move out on her own. Understanding her need for independence, they welcomed her decision. They had even given her a bonus to help her out with expenses for the new place.

Celia was impressed and a little jealous at Ursula's stroke of luck.

Celia asked, "How did you know to come?"

"My employers found your letter in their mailbox and gave it to me," Ursula said.

It had already been decided that Celia would stay with them until she figured out what to do next.

When they arrived at the apartment, Ursula helped Celia find a place to put her belongings. Then Ursula suggested to Celia that she take a nice, warm bath to relax.

After her bath, Celia made her way into the living room where Nando and Ursula sat talking.

"Feeling better?" Ursula asked.

Celia nodded and looked at Nando, who was staring at her.

"Do you feel like talking?"

"As a matter of fact, I do," Celia said.

Celia told them all about the horrors the Jameses had put her through. She cried as she told some of the most impossible to imagine mistreatments. Ursula and Nando had been beyond outraged and comforted Celia.

They offered again to let her stay with them, and she was grateful.

Weeks had gone by, and they all fell into a comfortable quiet routine. They each complemented each other very well. Nando did all the cooking. His meals were excellent. He had even taught Celia how to make a dish or two. But he was a terrible housekeeper.

Ursula had an excellent sense of color and taste. She had made their little apartment into something you see only in magazines.

Celia was good at finances, so she managed their expenses and budgeting. She was still clouded by the thought that she was not contributing financially, even when Ursula and Nando were quick to put her apprehension at ease.

"*No te preocupes*," they would tell her. "Something will come up soon."

And something did.

She had found a job in a radio-manufacturing company called Zenith. The company was located within walking distance of their apartment. She couldn't wait to get home to share the good news.

When she walked in to the apartment, she found Ursula and Nando seated at the table. They appeared to be reading something.

"I have wonderful news!" Celia beamed.

They looked up at Celia with serious faces.

"Who died?" Celia laughed.

Ursula looked at Nando, who put his head down, and then she looked at Celia.

She had regret written all over her delicate features.

"You're being sued," Ursula finally said.

3

The Jameses were suing Celia for breaching her contract. The court date was in two weeks' time.

Celia was extremely nervous. She had never been a part of anything like this, and it was all scary and intimidating.

She could not eat or sleep.

Ursula, noticing the decline in weight on Celia and fearing she may become ill, conferred with her mentor family about places she would be able to go for a small hiatus. As luck would have it, her *patrones* owned a small cottage home on the outskirts of the city.

They told Ursula that she and her family would be welcome to use it for as long as they needed.

Ursula spoke to Nando about it. He readily liked the idea, and they ambushed Celia with the decision to leave for the weekend.

Outnumbered, Celia gave in.

The trio packed everything they would need for the small trip and left Friday night after work.

On the drive there, Ursula and Nando sang silly songs. Their voices were horrible. Soon they had Celia laughing and joining them in their off-key melody.

By nine o'clock, they reached the cottage. It was the equivalent of five houses merged into one.

Nando shook his head as he helped take out the luggage. "This is the small cottage?"

"It's beautiful!" Ursula exclaimed.

"Oh wow!" Celia agreed.

They went inside and stood in the foyer, afraid to move an inch for fear of breaking anything.

Exquisite furniture, silk drapes, and ceramic pieces greeted their eyes. Yet there was still a "homey" feeling to the place.

It was a one-level home, and they easily found their way around. Excluding the four bathrooms, they counted at least seven bedrooms. All different sizes.

The bedrooms were located on either side of the house. Nando opted for a room on the left side of the house, as the women selected rooms on the right. He wanted to allow them some privacy.

Living in a small apartment, there is not a whole lot that remains private for them.

After everyone got refreshed and changed, Nando made small square sandwiches for everyone.

Celia and Ursula tried to figure out the fireplace and finally got it going. Winter was approaching, and the cottage was chilly.

They sat in a circle, eating sandwiches and drinking hot cocoa.

Celia closed her eyes. "Nando, what's in this? It's delicious!"

"Ummm…ham and cheese?" Nando responded with a laugh.

"This is not ham and cheese!" Celia responded, opening the sandwich and reviewing its contents.

"I promise you it is," Nando said, still amused.

"What did you put in it?" Celia asked unconvinced.

"Ummm…ham and cheese?" Nando repeated.

This warranted him a whack on the arm by Celia.

They all laughed.

They talk for a bit about current events in the news and different things from work. It was with silent understanding that the subject of Celia's hearing would not be a discussion they were having this weekend.

This was a time to relax and gain some much-needed strength for the days ahead.

Feeling tired, they cleaned up and headed to bed.

The cottage was built adjacent to an amazing lake. They had seen it on the drive up. The lake was within walking distance, so they decided that if it wasn't too cold tomorrow, they would have a minipicnic.

The next morning, Celia woke up before anyone else in the house. She headed to the kitchen to make coffee. She actually had a good night's rest and felt much better.

She thought of Ursula and Nando and smiled. They were so good to her.

"What are you smiling about?" Nando asked, startling her.

Celia jumped a bit. "You scared me!"

Nando came into the kitchen. "Well, I didn't mean to. You seemed far away."

"Well, if you must know, I was thinking that I'm very lucky to have you both. I'd be a mess without you."

Nando came to stand directly in front of Celia. "We are family, Celia. Hope you know that," Nando said seriously. "I've come to learn that family is not defined by blood. It's defined by those that stand by your side and support and love you."

Celia was touched by his words. "Thank you, Nando." Then she embraced him.

Nando welcomed her embrace. Her head barely reached his chest. He could smell her hair. It smelled like coconuts. He wondered what shampoo she used.

Celia never noticed how toned Nando was. *Geez, he was rock solid*, she thought.

She wondered if he had a girlfriend. She didn't think so. Ursula would've told her.

It felt warm and safe in his embrace. Without thinking, she squeezed him tighter.

Nando felt a sudden electric undercurrent in his body. Celia must have felt it too, because she immediately let him go.

"Um…I'm going to see if Ursula is awake so we can have breakfast," Celia said, all of a sudden extremely nervous.

When she left the kitchen, Nando had to steady himself and held on to the sink.

What just happened? he thought.

4

During breakfast, things went back to normal somewhat. Celia would catch Nando staring at her, and she would immediately look away.

Had his eyes always been that color? Celia thought as she shook her head. *What the hell was wrong with her?*

The day turned out to be beautiful. It was a tad windy, but the sun was out, and it felt perfect against their skin. They decided to pack a light lunch and head to the lake. Nando had found some bicycles in the garage and thought it would fun to ride them instead of walking.

Celia had never learned how to ride a bicycle. Nando volunteered to teach her.

Ursula was so excited she grabbed their lunch and put it in her bicycle basket and told Celia and Nando that she would see them at the lake.

Celia was a little nervous, but Nando reassured her that she would be fine. He held on to the seat of Celia's bicycle with one hand and with the other held on to the handle bar.

Celia held on to the handle bars and swiftly hopped on the bike. Nando had to quickly remove his hand before Celia sat on it.

"Okay, now I need you to look straight ahead," Nando explained. "Don't look down. Envision where you are going."

"Please don't let go of me," Celia pleaded.

Nando felt a tug in his heart. He looked at her. "Never."

Celia felt herself blushed.

"Now I am going to let go of the handle bar." Celia nodded.

"Pedal, Celia," Nando requested. "I am still holding the bottom of your seat."

As Celia pedaled, Nando jogged slowly by her side.

Celia gained momentum.

"Straight…Straight." Nando encouraged, still holding the back of the bicycle.

"Nando, I'm doing it! I'm doing it," Celia exclaimed. Unfortunately, she took a quick look at Nando and drove straight into a bush.

Celia burst in laughter. "Oh my, I'm so sorry."

Nando helped her get the bicycle back on the road. "Okay, let's try this again."

Celia noticed he wasn't smiling. *Boy, he took things seriously*, she thought.

Not wanting to disappoint him, she got back on the bicycle.

"Remember what I told you. Look ahead," Nando said.

It took Celia four more attempts to keep the bicycle straight without winding up in the bushes. Between her shoe falling off and seeing a turtle on the road and a fly going into her mouth, Celia was sure that Nando was regretting to have ever volunteered to teach her.

When she gained momentum and Nando felt confident that Celia had finally figured her balance on the bicycle, he let go of the seat.

Celia made it about five feet before she had realized that Nando was not beside her. She became insecure all over again and hit the brakes hard. The bicycle came to a jerked stop, and Celia went flying off.

"Celia! Are you all right?" Nando yelled, rushing to Celia.

Celia was holding her knee. "You let me go! You said you wouldn't let me go!" Nando felt like a jackass.

"Let me see your knee," he commanded.

Celia removed her hand and cringed when she saw that her knee was bleeding. This was her first scrape ever.

Nando took his handkerchief out of his pocket and placed it on Celia's knee. "Can you walk?"

"I'm not sure…Let's try it," Celia said.

He helped her get up, and she cringed. "I'll live."

"Let's get to the house. The owners should have some antiseptic or something," Nando reasoned.

Nando held on to Celia's elbow while she limped back to the house.

They entered through the kitchen. "Wait here," Nando asked.

He came back a few minutes later with tons of cotton and some antiseptic. He looked around, as if trying to decide something. He placed the items on the counter, and then without warning, he picked up Celia and lowered her very gently on the counter.

Celia was embarrassed. All she managed to say was, "Oh."

Nando grabbed the antiseptic and cotton. He then looked at Celia and asked, "May I?"

"Oh sure," Celia answered with fake confidence.

Celia watched Nando work in a very slow and deliberate manner to clean her knee. She looked at his hands. She noticed they were slightly rough. His hands spoke volumes of his work ethic.

She then looked at his arms, and her eyes traveled all the way up his biceps. She could see the outline of his muscles through his shirt.

His head was down, so she looked at his hair. He had thick beautiful black hair.

Well, she thought, *at least my children will not be bald. Wait! What? Children?* She must be more stressed out than she originally thought.

She was like a kid sister to him. She figured he would go for more "worldly women." They would be taller for sure and definitely sophisticated.

Her perfect skin now had a nasty scrape that would definitely leave a mark. He felt so stupid.

Why did he let her go? he thought.

She had been through so much already. At the very least he could've taught her how to ride a bicycle without causing her pain.

Celia had realized that Nando looked intense and perhaps…guilty? She did accuse him of letting her go. "Nando…?" she began. "I am okay. This is just a little scrape."

Nando just nodded but never looked at Celia.

Celia tried again. "I'm sorry I was ugly to you earlier. It was my fault. I wasn't paying attention."

"Yeah, well, it should've never happened," Nando said sadly.

"But it did and it's okay. I'm okay."

"We are done here. I'm going to put this cloth band over it. We'll check on it later," Nando said.

"Okay," was all Celia could answer.

"Ready?" Nando extended his arms to help Celia down from the counter.

Celia placed her hands on Nando's shoulders while he held her by her waist.

Being careful not to touch her knee, he slowly lifted her and lowered her onto the ground.

He didn't immediately let her go. His lingering caused Celia to look up at Nando.

For a brief moment as they looked into each other's eyes, Celia felt an undercurrent of electricity, and she shivered.

"Are you cold?" Nando asked but still holding on to Celia's waist.

Celia couldn't find her voice. But it was unnecessary as Ursula came barging in the kitchen. "Where have you been? What took you guys so long?

Ursula looked from Celia to Nando and then back again.

Nando, realizing he was still holding Celia, let her go immediately. "We had a little incident. Celia got hurt."

"What? Hurt? How?" Ursula asked alarmingly and walked over to Celia.

"It's nothing, Ursula. See? Just a scrape," Celia answered while showing her knee to Ursula for further inspection.

Satisfied, Ursula sighed loudly. "Do we still want to head to the lake? I brought the food back…"

Celia, not wanting to ruin the day, agreed to head to the lake.

Nando tried to propose that they all stay indoors, but Celia was adamant that they go.

So they left once again, save this time they walked.

Celia could feel her knee throbbing but put on a brave front.

And as it turned out, they all had a great time.

Nando was finally able to relax and smile. He even poked fun at Celia by imitating her bicycle riding to Ursula.

They all had a good laugh, and after a couple of hours, they decided to head on back to the cottage.

This was their last day at the cottage. They were headed back home tomorrow early in the morning.

Feeling that Celia needed to rest, Nando proposed that she sit and relax while he and Ursula made supper.

Celia agreed immediately. She had not realized how tired she was.

When Nando came to get Celia for dinner, he found her fast asleep on the sofa. He was overwhelmed by feelings of tenderness for her.

He debated whether or not to move her. The sofa actually looked uncomfortable, but she looked peaceful.

Ursula came in and noticed Celia too. "Poor thing. She's exhausted."

Ursula left the room and came back with a pillow and quilt. With Nando's help, she placed the pillow under Celia's head, and Nando covered her with the quilt.

"I'll go serve our food. I'm starving," Ursula said and walked back into the kitchen.

Nando looked at Celia's peaceful face and impulsively bent over and kissed her forehead.

5

She bewitched him.

She was the missing piece to his soul. In their time together, he had come to love and respect her.

She seemed so strong in the face of adversity, and yet all he wanted to do was hold her in his arms and tell her it was all going to be fine.

He saw straight through her façade. It was much like his own. One had to appear strong because, when it came down to it, weaklings were devoured.

Nando had come to court with Celia to offer his support.

Looking at her now so poised, graceful, and proud made his heart ache for the injustice of it all—the Jameses on one side with their high-rate attorneys and Celia on the other side all alone. The scene had been a replica of David versus Goliath.

Against advisement, Celia had refused council. She felt her strength was in her truth and in the conviction that wrong would never prevail over what's right. Because there was a contract and under the law it was binding, Celia had hoped to appeal to the judge's sense of morality.

The judge had appeared deeply disturbed with Celia's account of her time with the Jameses. Upon cross examination from one of the Jameses' lawyers, she held her own and didn't allow herself to be intimidated.

The judge had said nothing afterward and ordered a recess.

"Are you holding up okay?" Nando asked when Celia walked outside.

"I've been better," she responded.

"Are you hungry? I brought some sandwiches," Nando said.

"I couldn't eat, Nando. I'm too nervous."

They sat in silence and waited for the judge to come back. Nando noticed that Celia had worn the necklace of the Virgin Mary of the Sacred Heart that her friends from Puerto Rico had gifted her.

Seeing her so sad and worried, Nando wished he could've traded places with her.

After thirty-five minutes, they were ordered back inside.

The judge sat down and, for a moment, appeared as if he had tasted something bad.

He cleared his throat and stated the following:

"It is inconceivable to me that one human being would freely and with malice treat another so viciously. For it is my understanding that we are all God's creatures and thus created equal. This girl came to you, ignorant of the language, living in a strange city, filled with hope, and you took advantage. You single-handedly shattered her trust and, what's worse, tried to destroy her spirit. And for that, you shall forever feel ashamed.

"Under the law, I'm obliged to enforce agreements between parties. Having read the contract that was signed and agreed upon by both Priscilla and Milton James and this young lady, I find that said contract is null and void.

"The contract stipulates that "a girl" shall live and work in the residence of the plaintiffs, that the plaintiffs are obliged to pay this girl for services rendered. They are also obliged to provide time off for worship and personal endeavors and so forth. For these stipulations alone, she could be suing you!

"Unfortunately, for my determination, that would not be possible because it is not apparent to me that "a girl" that was hired by the Jameses is "the girl" standing here before me. Her name is nowhere on this document. Sure, a signature bearing the name of the defendant does appear, but who's to say that she was the one who signed? It is so determined by me that "the girl" hired could've been just about anyone! Therefore, all charges are dismissed!"

The judge rapped his gravel and stood up.

Celia looked back at a smiling Nando. He gave her the thumbs-up.

She looked over to the Jameses. Milton was talking to one of the lawyers. By the look on their faces, it had not appeared to be a pleasant conversation. Patricia was

165

standing with her hands crossed in front of her. She looked over at Celia, and the women stared at one another.

Patricia then smiled and winked at Celia.

The gesture gave Celia the chills.

Celia collected her belongings and made her way out of the courtroom where Nando waited patiently.

On impulse, she ran to him.

Nando readily opened his arms to welcome her. The embrace felt just right and natural.

He had never felt this way about anyone in his life. He wanted so much to kiss her, but he refrained.

Celia could never love a man like him.

He was an uneducated fool, and she deserved better.

6

Celia had a suitor.

His name was Ethan Tracy.

Ethan was a jewelry designer and owner of one of the largest boutiques in Chicago—and would be soon opening another outlet in New York City.

The outbreak of WWII diminished the production of the jewelry industry in Europe. Imports to the United States of precious metals such as platinum and gold were almost unobtainable and rationed. This forced jewelers to start using semiprecious stones.

Ethan's designs were one of the kind and highly sought after by the rich and famous, making him very successful in his field. He was also very well educated. Having completed his business degree somewhere in Europe, he returned to Chicago to start his business.

Ethan was very handsome. He had blue eyes, a cleft chin, and a smile that could've melted ice. In addition to being impeccably dressed at all times and constantly in the society pages mingling with the "creme de la crème," he was said to be the most eligible bachelor.

He could've had any girl he wanted, but he wanted Celia.

Celia couldn't figure out why.

She was not worldly and refined like the girls she saw him with in the newspapers. Furthermore, she had no money.

Nonetheless, every day Ethan walked her home and came upstairs for a cup of coffee.

It might have been improper, save for the fact that Ursula and Nando were home by the time Celia got off work.

Ethan sat at their table and told them the latest in gossip from the socialites.

He had a way with words and always made Ursula and Celia laugh with his vivid descriptions. He impressed them with his humbleness.

Nando never stuck around when Ethan visited.

Celia was torn. She was in love with a man who would never see her as anything more than a kid sister.

She was in love with Nando.

No one knew, not even Ursula.

Celia had never known anyone like Nando.

His sense of integrity and loyalty were overwhelming. He made her want to be the best person possible. She wanted him to be proud of her. She wanted to share with him all of her hopes and dreams. But maybe a woman like

Celia was not what Nando aspired too. Maybe he didn't want an equal in poverty.

That was understandable.

Hoping against hope that Nando would show her the least bit of interest, she turned to Ethan.

She wanted a family, and Ethan seemed to want that too.

Tonight he asked her if he could kiss her. Celia had hesitated but then agreed.

His kiss was soft and gentle.

This had been her first kiss, and she was disappointed.

She had expected shivers or goosebumps or a lightning bolt to strike her...anything at all. Nothing.

Boy, those *telenovelas* she watched with Ursula were highly deceitful and greatly exaggerated, she thought.

She told Ursula that night about the kiss, and Ursula giggled. She thought Ethan was to die for.

She chastised Celia for not being more flirtatious. "*Chica*, if you continue being so proper, he may get tired and lose interest in you," she said.

"Then let him. I'm not going to stop being who I am," Celia responded.

And so Ethan continued to walk Celia home and come upstairs for his usual cup of coffee.

Then one day after work, he wasn't waiting for Celia as usual.

This struck her as strange. She wondered if everything was all right as she walked home by herself.

When she got home, Ursula asked, "Where's Ethan?"

169

"I have no idea. He never showed up after work," Celia replied.

Nando had come out of the kitchen then, and Celia could've sworn he looked relieved.

They had a quiet supper, and shortly past eight o' clock, the doorbell rang.

"Who can it be at this hour?" Nando asked to no one specifically.

He opened the door to find Ethan on the other side.

Nando asked him to come in.

"Hi! We missed you today," Ursula said.

"What about you, Celia? Did you miss me?" Ethan asked as he approached Celia.

"Of course!" was all she could say.

"Well, good, because I have something I've been meaning to ask you, and I'm glad you are all here."

Ethan took Celia's hands, brought them to his lips, and kissed them. "In all my life, I would have never imagined meeting someone as terrific as you, Celia. I didn't meet you today after work because I was getting something for you."

He took a deep breath.

It was very obvious that Ethan was nervous. He had started to sweat profusely.

Then much to everyone's surprise, he then got on one knee and said the words she knew were coming. "Would you marry me?"

Celia looked down to his hands. He was holding the biggest sapphire ring she had ever seen.

Celia stood motionless. She had decided that if he proposed she would accept.

Now here she was…looking at Ethan, and all she could think of was…those big droplets of sweat falling down the sides of his face. She couldn't concentrate.

She wanted more than anything to tell him to wipe his face.

He must have heard the inner voice inside her brain, because Ethan let go of one of her hands and reached into his breast pocket. He retrieved a handkerchief and then wiped his face.

Ethan looked at Celia expectantly.

Celia took a deep breath, looked into Ethan's beautiful eyes, and responded.

7

The minute Ethan had gotten on his knees, Nando was out of the apartment.

He couldn't take it. He had felt like he had a ton of bricks on his chest.

He had lost her.

Nando headed toward the train station. He was going nowhere specific.

He just needed to get away and think.

The station was almost deserted.

He got on a train and was relieved that only one other person was in the cart.

He sat in the corner and started to cry.

He could see Celia's face. It was the only face he could remember every detail of when he closed his eyes.

He couldn't begrudge her marrying Ethan. He was everything Nando wasn't.

He knew Ethan had good intentions and would make Celia happy.

He had lost all track of time. It was 1:00 a.m. He had no idea where he was at this point.

Nando figured he get off at the next stop and head back.

When the train stopped, Nando got off, went around, and waited on the other side of the platform.

A group of teens came up the platform where Nando sat waiting for the train to arrive. Not wanting to look the part of a victim, he stood up and started walking.

"Hey! Where ya going?" one of the boys said.

Nando kept walking.

"Wait up, man. Are you scared?" another boy said.

Nando kept walking.

The teens picked up their pace and caught up with him and blocked his path.

"What do we have here?" one asked. "If it isn't a fucking wet bag!"

Nando looked at the teens. He counted five. *Contraya'o!* Damn! He was outnumbered.

"Here, take my moni. I don wan no troble," Nando said as he threw his wallet on the ground in front of the group.

"I don wan no troble," they mimicked and laughed.

The first one poked Nando in the chest and said, "Listen, man, why don't you go back to your own country?"

The only thing Nando could think of was to say, "I am no Mexican. I Puerto Rican."

"Same difference, amigo. You don't belong here!"

The boys pushed Nando around.

He figured he would keep calm. Let them have their fun, and they would get bored and leave.

Nando never saw it coming.

He felt something painful in between his eyes. He put his hands up to his face.

His hands became wet. He saw blood.

His vision blurred, and he fell to the ground.

Somewhere in the distance, he heard a whistle. *The train must be coming*, he thought.

People running…a scream…then darkness.

Nando had been stabbed with a screwdriver.

8

The call came shortly after 3:00 a.m.

As they drove to the hospital in a taxicab, Ursula and Celia cried and prayed. The only thing they had been told over the phone was that Nando had been badly hurt.

When they arrived, they were advised of what had happened.

Nando had lost a lot of blood. The outlook was bleak.

They couldn't see him yet, but were promised that a doctor would come out and give them an update.

And so they waited.

If she could take it all back, Celia thought. She had always followed her heart.

Seeing Ethan on his knees proposing marriage was not what she wanted.

Celia knew he could give her all the material possessions in the world, but all she wanted was Nando.

She realized that, even if Nando never wanted her, she had to be true to herself.

Marrying Ethan would have been a mistake.

So she turned him down.

She should have told Nando that she loved him. Why? Why didn't she? She asked herself.

She looked at Ursula. Her friend looked so pale.

Celia had seen the bond between brother and sister. She knew without a shadow of a doubt that if Ursula were to lose her brother, life would be meaningless.

Ursula looked up at Celia and smiled through her tears. "You know, I had my doubts all along. You never said anything to me, so I figured you didn't feel the same way he does. But tonight, you confirmed what I had long suspected."

Celia frowned in confusion. She didn't know if she was tired or what, but Ursula was rambling. "What? What are you talking about?" she asked.

Ursula rolled her eyes. "When were you ever going to tell me that you we in love with my brother?"

Celia opened her eyes wide. "How did you...?" she began to ask.

"It's written all over your face." Ursula interrupted.

Celia looked down, embarrassed.

Then something struck her, and she looked at Ursula. "What did you mean by you figured I didn't feel the same way he does?"

Ursula placed her hands on her friend's shoulders. "Celia, he loves you! Nando is in love with you!"

All that wasted time.

The implications of that simple truth were too much to bear, Celia thought. What if she lost him?

The women put their heads together and held hands.

"What if…?" Celia began.

"Ssshhh. Don't…please…don't even think about it!" Ursula said.

9

They had been in the waiting room for four hours when the doctor finally came by.

He explained that the screwdriver missed Nando's brain by a quarter of an inch. It was a miracle that he was still alive.

Because he had lost a lot of blood, they were going to keep him in the hospital for a few days.

"Can we see him?" asked Ursula.

"Yes, one at a time," the doctor urged. "He's awake now but very drowsy. Keep it brief."

Celia let Ursula go in first.

By the time it was her turn, Nando had fallen asleep.

The entire top of his head was covered in bandages. His eyes were so swollen you could barely see them.

Celia held Nando's hand in her own and cried.

She felt him squeeze her hand. She looked up to find him watching her.

"I thought you were asleep," she said.

"And miss seeing you? Never." He smiled then. "If I had to put toothpicks under my eyelids to keep them open for you, I would."

"Hey, are you crying?"

Celia couldn't stop the free flow of tears. The thought of never seeing him again…

"I'm okay, Celia." Then he couldn't contain himself. "Is your fiancée here with you?"

Celia shook her head no.

"Oh…"

The most awaited and unexpected words for Nando came next.

"Nando…I love you," Celia whispered.

Nando closed his eyes.

He had finally fallen asleep, she thought.

She slowly let go of his hand, then turned around to leave.

"I love you too, Celia."

Everything was going to be all right.

10

Six weeks later, Nando came home.

The doctor said he would always have a scar where the screwdriver broke into the skin, but other than that he would be able to resume his life as usual.

Ever so shyly, both Celia and Nando had disclosed their true feelings about each other and planned for the future they never thought possible.

It still amazed them both how they wanted the same things out of life.

And the first time when Nando kissed Celia, she wasn't struck by lightning as she had hoped; but instead, the earth trembled, her legs grew weak, and she felt so dizzy she almost passed out in Nando's arms.

Nothing about their lives had been "normal." They had both experienced things that had forced them to grow up way too soon. But they both had discussed and felt that some traditions were worth holding on to. So they had decided to wait until after they were married to make love.

It was the hardest thing they ever had to do.

Nando had begun putting money aside to buy a ring for Celia. He knew Celia didn't care for material possessions and meant it when she told him that she didn't need nor wanted anything fancy. Celia will finally be his wife and the mother of his children. He loved her so much, and she deserved nothing but the best from him.

Celia never imagined that such powerful love ever existed. She wished she could've talked to her mother—heard her voice and her laughter. She wished she would've been able to ask her for advice.

"I'm going to be okay, Momma," Celia had whispered to herself, knowing without a doubt that Nando would be by her side regardless of what life threw at them.

Ursula couldn't be happier for the both of them. Nando had confessed to her long ago about his love for Celia. She had encouraged her brother to say something sooner, but he felt he was not good enough for her. Ursula had tried to talk to Celia about Nando and see if she felt the same, but by then she had already introduced them to Ethan.

Everything was falling into place, and the trio couldn't have been happier.

Days later, they all received a surprise.

Nando, Celia, and Ursula were sitting on the living room floor playing cards, eating pizza, and accusing one another of cheating at the game when the doorbell rang.

"Wonder who it is?" Nando asked as he got up. "It's not your boyfriend again?" he chided Celia and kissed her on the forehead.

"Maybe...," Celia responded, batting her eyelashes.

When Nando opened the door, standing before him smiling was none other than...Guillermo.

11

Nando could not believe his eyes!

He thought he would never see his friend again. "How is this possible?" Nando asked in amazement as he embraced Guillermo.

"Come in! Come in!"

Guillermo walked into their apartment and hugged Ursula. "*Ay Dio mio*! You are even more beautiful than when I last saw you. How is that possible?"

Ursula appropriately blushed and hugged Guillermo back. "You flirt," she said in between laughs.

"Oh, I was not the one with *la reputacion*...," Guillermo said and pointed at Nando. "That one over there is...well, was the dangerous one with the ladies."

They all laughed except for Celia.

Nando saw her expression and promptly went over to appease her. "No one but you now, my love."

"Better not be," Celia responded with mock anger.

"So how did you find us?" asked Nando, still surprised to see his childhood friend standing in their living room.

"It was all her," Guillermo answered, pointing to Celia.

Nando and Ursula were more confused than ever. "Celia? How?" they asked in unison.

So Celia explained how Guillermo also happened to be working for Zenith. They were in different divisions of the company, so she had never seen or met him before.

Guillermo recently got promoted and had the same schedule as Celia. They will later meet in the cafeteria during their lunchtime and strike up a conversation.

They soon realized their connection, and the rest, as they say, was history.

Just when they thought things couldn't get any better, they were proved wrong.

Guillermo and Nando stayed up talking long after the women had gone to bed. They had a lot to catch up on.

Nando wanted to know what happened to Guillermo after they last saw each other at the train station.

Guillermo explained to Nando that he had sat at the station that night, wondering what to do. He was so tired and exhausted he had not realized he had fallen asleep.

He would be awoken by a police officer asking him to vacate the premises lest he be arrested for vagrancy. He readily agreed and started walking up the stairs to go back to the street.

Guillermo stated that the police officer, for some reason, followed him up the stairs. At the time, Guillermo had thought he had changed his mind and was going to arrest him. Instead he told him that if he was looking for a job, his brother-in-law worked loading and unloading merchandise for various retail locations.

The police officer who introduced himself as Nicholas gave Guillermo the address of where he needed to go. He told Guillermo to ask for Jose Santos.

He then asked Guillermo where he was from. Guillermo responded that he was born and raised in Puerto Rico. The officer then volunteered that his wife and her family were from Cuba.

Cuba is the largest island of the Caribbean; and, much like the Puerto Ricans, Cubans immigrated in search of a better way of life.

The officer then told Guillermo that he knew a friend at a nearby shelter and he would be able to get him in for the night.

The next day, Guillermo spoke with Sr. Santos and got the job on a trial basis. He slept in various shelters in the meantime, and after a month, he had managed to save enough to rent a room in a small family house.

The house belonged to a young couple who just had a baby. Renting the extra room would help the couple out financially until the wife would be able to return to work.

Later, he heard about Zenith doing a mass hiring as they were about to expand from radio manufacturing to televisions.

Guillermo took a chance in coming to Chicago with the hopes of getting hired. And he did.

Guillermo told Nando that he knew about his relationship with Celia. "She is phenomenal, Nando. She has brains and beauty for sure! A real little firecracker too!"

Nando actually turned red as his friend patted him on the back. "Congratulations, my dear brother…congratulations."

12

It was Celia's birthday.

Today she was turning nineteen years old. She didn't feel nineteen at all, she thought. So many things have happened in this last year that at times she wondered what else was in store for her. Nonetheless, she was looking forward to her life.

She was no longer alone.

Ignoring Celia's protests, Nando wanted to have a celebratory dinner, and he wanted to cook the meal himself. Ursula had been placed in charge of the birthday cake.

Guillermo had been invited and was told to be at the apartment by seven o'clock.

At exactly six thirty, Celia walked through the door of the apartment to find Guillermo already there. "You are early! Must be hungry!"

"Hey, where there is food, there is a Puerto Rican!" Guillermo answered with a laugh.

When Celia made her way into the dining room, she stopped dead in her tracks.

She could not believe what she was seeing.

There were candles everywhere! She looked up and saw an array of sheer fabrics crisscrossed from the ceiling, creating the illusion of a canopy. It was the most magical sight Celia had ever seen. Nando stood at the far end of the table next to Ursula. He was dressed in a suit and was holding a bouquet of white roses.

Something familiar caught Celia's eye on the table. Encased in a white ivory frame was the only picture of her mother, Iluminada.

Celia looked over at Ursula. "I'm sorry, Celia, for going through your things, but we felt your mom should be part of this moment with you."

And as if on cue, Nando stepped forward until he was standing in front of Celia and got on one knee. He looked at Celia with tears in his eyes and a heart overflowing with all the love he felt for her. "Celia, will you be my wife?"

Nando presented her with a diamond solitaire ring.

Celia couldn't see. Her vision had been blurred by tears.

She blinked and wiped her eyes with the sleeve of her dress.

She looked at Guillermo and then at Ursula, who were both grinning from ear to ear.

She then looked at Nando. Her handsome Nando.

And simply said, "Yes."

At that precise moment, a gust of air was felt in the room and all the candles blew out, save for one. An intense scent permeated the room instantly.

It was the scent of lilies.

And then Celia knew her mother would always be with her.

Epilogue

After five years together, she was still the most beautiful woman he had ever seen.

Nando watched Celia tuck their youngest daughter, Anastacia, in bed.

He looked over at his oldest daughter, Beatriz, already sleeping peacefully and smiled.

He contemplated the three. His girls.

This is all he ever wanted.

Celia and Nando had gotten married in a quiet ceremony, with only Guillermo and Ursula in attendance as their witnesses.

Nando surprised Celia with a dress he bought from a boutique. He had seen her eyeing it with longing when they had passed by the shop one weekend. He understood that in another life, her father would have been the one to purchase the dress for her. But that was not how it was meant to be for Celia. So he had then decided that he would put in some extra hours at work to get it for her.

He would never forget her face when he saw her in the dress and wearing her mother's pearls.

He knew of the significance of the necklace and was touched that she had chosen that day to wear them.

Celia was promoted and given a hefty raise, and soon they were able to afford to move to a larger apartment. They were also able to purchase another car.

Guillermo and Nando qualified for a small business loan and opened a small restaurant. They felt inspired by many fellow Puerto Ricans who traveled down the road of independence and proved to be successful. They were in the "land of opportunity," and the time was prime for their venture.

They appropriately named their restaurant Mi Familia.

Ursula did the entire interior decorating for the restaurant; and realizing she may have some potential, she enrolled in college.

Celia handled the financial aspects of the business.

Wanting to quench her thirst for knowledge, Celia also enrolled in Private Investigator School. She hadn't been sure as to why this appealed to her and wondered if Salvador Morelli had influence her somehow.

The flexible hours of the restaurant had allowed Celia to continue working at Zenith during the day while Nando cared for their daughters. He was a strong but gentle father, and Beatriz and Anastacia adored him.

Opening night of the restaurant was the beginning of a prosperous venture for all of them. The Hispanic community, always proving to be avid supporters of their fellow Boricuas, came together and celebrated.

Word spread, and soon Mi Familia had earned a solid reputation for serving the best Puerto Rican food in town.

Nando had come home early from the restaurant. He never grew tired of how his heart warmed at the sight of his family. He was in awe of his wife. She was courageous and driven. She was a great mother. But more so, she made him a better man—a man he never thought he could be.

Celia had finished tucking the girls in. She walked over to Nando.

Hand in hand, they walked to their bedroom.

"I have something to tell you," Celia said.

"About Guillermo and Ursula?" Nando asked.

"Wait! You knew?" she asked disbelievingly. Ursula had confided the week before that she and Guillermo were in love. Celia thought it had been wonderful news. They were a perfect match.

"Of course!" Nando replied, "Guillermo told me he was going to propose this weekend and asked for my blessing."

"He's going to propose?" shouted Celia.

"Sshh, you'll wake up the girls!" Nando hushed.

Then he warned, "You can't tell her, Celia!"

"I wasn't going to!" Celia said while grabbing a pillow and hitting Nando upside his head.

Nando grabbed another pillow and hit Celia back on her arm. They both laughed.

As they lay in bed, whispering to each other about their day, Nando embraced his wife. He marveled at how perfectly her body fit in his embrace. He never thought happiness like this even existed. He was complete.

Celia got lost in the scent of her husband. She thought of how one determined individual could accomplish anything they set their minds to. But glory isn't such if it isn't shared with another person.

Celia and Nando knew that times of adversity would crane its ugly head from time to time. That was life. But in the end of it all, what doesn't break us…makes us stronger.

Glossary

- *nena*: term of endearment for "girl"
- *quenepas*: genip; caribbean fruit with green leathery skin and sweet and juicy pulp
- *cabrona*: technically meaning "goat" but used as a slang word to call a woman "slut" or "bitch"
- *guayabera*: men's shirt; typically distinguished by two vertical rows of closely sewn pleats that run the length of the front and back of the shirt
- *Dios te bendiga*: God bless you.
- *Anjeles te protejan siempre*: Angels protect you always.
- *'mija*: abbreviation for "mi hija" or "my daughter"
- *amiga*: female friend
- *Ay fuchilas*: slang for gross, yuck, pew
- *maldito desgraciado*: damn disgrace

- *maricon*: slang for "homosexual"
- *mamacita*: "little mother" but it's used to call a woman "sexy"
- *Hablas espanol*: Do you speak Spanish?
- *Que bien*: Very good.
- *patrones*: bosses
- *Apurate*: Hurry.
- *Gracias*: Thank you.
- *No te preocupes*: Don't worry.
- *telenovelas*: soap operas
- *reputacion*: reputation
- *mi famila*: my family
- *Boricuas*: native from Borinquen, which is the original name of Puerto Rico
- *Estas loco?* Are you crazy?

CPSIA information can be obtained
at www.ICGtesting.com
Printed in the USA
LVOW04s2054120816
500060LV00016B/171/P